CARLY'S FREEDOM

ANNIE HUTCHISON

Carly's Freedom

Copyright © 2024 by Annie Hutchison

A Sophron Press Imprint

All rights reserved.

No part of this publication may be reproduced, distributed, or transmitted in any form or by any means, including photocopying, recording, or other electronic or mechanical methods, without the prior written permission of the publisher, except as permitted by U.S. copyright law. For permission requests, email contact@anniehutchison.com

The story, all names, characters, and incidents portrayed in this production are fictitious. No identification with actual persons (living or deceased), places, buildings, and products is intended or should be inferred.

1st edition 2024

Contents

Dedication Page

This book is dedicated to all the women who have felt trapped by the trauma of sexual abuse. My prayer is that you would encounter the soul-freedom that comes from knowing how deeply and perfectly loved you are by Jesus Christ. Jesus died to give you victor's robes; you need only shed your rags of victimhood to receive them.

A special thank you to Mardi Shortridge and Melody Fitzsimmons for taking the time to catch my plethora of mistakes and helping me polish this book so that it is intelligible.

To my incredible husband Nate, thank you for your support, listening ear, and constant encouragement. I could not have written this book without you as my rock.

Preface

Why Christians Should Read a Book about Sexual Trauma

Carly's Freedom is a fictional story about the trauma one teenage girl faces when she learns that she has been the victim of digital sex trafficking.

According to the Polaris Project, "the crime of human trafficking does not require any movement whatsoever. Survivors can be recruited and trafficked in their own home towns, even their own homes." (Quote taken on August 22, 2024 from https://polarisproject.org/myths-facts-and-statistics/)

In my novel, Carly's experience of becoming a victim to the predatory nature of the pornography industry takes place without her knowledge or consent and without her ever realizing she had placed herself in a vulnerable situation until the damage had already been done.

In my time working as a high school teacher, I witnessed firsthand how teenagers driven by hormones and offered no helpful parental guidance would often take their own "nudes" (pictures of their exposed bodies) only to have their nakedness exposed in humiliating or threatening ways.

I witnessed a high school student stay in an abusive relationship with her boyfriend because he threatened to post her images to all of his contacts on social media if she ever left him. Additionally, I witnessed another young woman have her entire reputation destroyed because the boy she was dating got her to perform a sexual act on him at school while his friend secretly filmed the act. The two boys later posted this video for all of their Instagram and Snapchat friends to see.

While these two instances were both reported to officials and the teenage girls were offered every bit of support possible, the damage to their mental, emotional, and spiritual health was already done and their lives were permanently changed.

While Carly's Freedom is a fictional story, it represents the heartache that 81% of women face after being sexually harassed or assaulted (Statistic found on August 22, 2024 from https://www.nsvrc.org/resource/facts-behind-metoo-movement-national-study-sexual-harassment-and-assault).

Additionally, Carly's story, while unique in some details, is far more common than many people want to admit and her age of being 15-16 when the crimes were committed is also consistent with victim statistics presented in the Polaris Analysis of 2021 Data. In 2021, it was estimated that 30% of all victims of forced sex labor were minors.

Now you may be wondering why I would choose to write a book in the category of Christian Fiction that deals with sexual trauma. Below are just some reasons why this topic is relevant to the Church and needs to be addressed within Christian communities.

13 Mind-Blowing Statistics About Pornography and The Church

1. Over 40 million Americans are regular visitors to porn sites. The average visit lasts 6 minutes and 29 seconds

2. There are around 42 million porn websites, which totals around 370 million pages of porn.

3. The porn industry's annual revenue is more than the NFL, NBA, and MLB combined. It is also more than the combined revenues of ABC, CBS, and NBC.

4. 47% of families in the United States reported that pornography is a problem in their home. Pornography use increases the marital infidelity rate by more than 300%.

5. 11 is the average age that a child is first exposed to porn, and 94% of children will see porn by the age of 14.

6. 56% of American divorces involve one party having an "obsessive interest" in pornographic websites.

7. 70% of Christian youth pastors report that they have had at least one teen come to them for help in dealing with pornography in the past 12 months.

8. 68% of church-going men and over 50% of pastors view porn on a regular basis. Of young Christian adults 18-24 years old, 76% actively search for porn.

9. 59% of pastors said that married men seek their help for porn use.

10. 33% of women aged 25 and under search for porn at least once per month.

11. Only 13% of self-identified Christian women say they never watch porn—87% of Christian women have watched porn.

12. 55% of married men and 25% of married women say they watch porn at least once a month.

13. 57% of pastors say porn addiction is the most damaging issue in their congregation. 69% say porn has adversely impacted the church.

(Statistics found on August 22, 2024 from https://www.missionfrontiers.org/issue/article/15-mind-blowing-statistics-about-pornography-and-the-church#:~:text=8.,76%25%20actively%20search%20for%20porn)

Please remember that any consumption of pornographic content means that human souls were shattered and many lives were ruined for your sexual gratification. Engaging in porn also has devastating effects on your conscience, your relationship with God, and your relationship with your spouse/future spouse. It is my deepest prayer and wish that as a Christian community, we can set the example of how to keep our eyes and hearts pure so that stories like Carly's become less commonplace.

If you or someone you know needs help to quit porn, please consider visiting

https://www.covenanteyes.com/how-it-works/#pricing-section

https://puredesire.org/resources/

If you would like to learn more about this issue or make a difference and join the fight against sex trafficking and the sex industry, please consider visiting

https://www.awoministries.org/what-we-do

https://www.rahab-ministries.org/volunteer/

https://www.lovesarmoutreach.org/programs

https://ourrescue.org/join-the-fight

https://rescue1global.org/about-us/why-rescue-1/

"For this is the will of God, your sanctification: that you abstain from sexual immorality; that each one of you knows how to control his own body in holiness and honor, not in the passion of lust like the Gentiles who do not know God; that no one transgress and wrong his brother in this matter, because the Lord is an avenger in all these things, as we told you beforehand and solemnly warned you. For God has not called us for impurity, but in holiness. Therefore whoever disregards this, disregards not man but God, who gives his Holy Spirit to you." 1 Thessalonians 4:3-8 ESV

Prologue

When Carly Learns the Truth

J unior year of high school was off to a great start, and Carly was delighted to find that so many guys were paying attention to her.

"Looking good!" Josh cat-called from across the hall. Carly blushed as she tried to act annoyed.

In her second period class, Kyle Belfi, the newly named captain of the football team, sat next to her and flirted surreptitiously most of the class time while the teacher wasn't looking at them.

Carly had thought that after the abrupt way her first and only boyfriend, Ryan, had dumped her, she would never be able to feel nervous flutters in her stomach about a boy again, but Kyle was funny and seemed really sweet.

As Carly was about to get on the school bus, she saw Kyle running towards her. "Carly, wait up a sec!" he shouted.

Carly stepped back from the bus and turned toward Kyle. "What's up?" she asked.

"Why don't you let me drive you home? I only live a couple blocks away; it would be no trouble." Kyle grinned his handsome smile as he looked down into her eyes. Carly felt that flutter of excitement again, but knew her mother would kill her if some hotshot football player she barely knew drove her home on the first day of school.

She smiled up at him, "Sorry, Kyle. My mom has some pretty strict rules, and catching rides with a practical stranger is one of them." Carly pouted her lower lip before getting onto the bus.

The next day, in second period, Kyle told her that they were going to become good friends, and that eventually her mom would be begging for him to drive Carly home after school. Carly laughed. He certainly seemed determined to win her good opinion and most definitely wanted to date her.

For the next four months, Kyle flirted with Carly in their Spanish class, and chose to bring a few football buddies to the area where she and her friends ate lunch so that they could get to be good friends.

Even though Kyle had been friends with her ex-boyfriend Ryan, she had never spent any time with him. In fact, as Carly reflected back on her relationship with Ryan, she realized that he never introduced her to any of his friends. They always spent time alone or with her friends and family. Carly had thought that she would marry Ryan someday because he had always told her he would love her forever. He had given her a beautiful silver ring with a tiny opal in it as a promise ring. Ryan had made her feel like his princess and when he took her to his senior prom, Carly felt that it was the perfect time to give herself to him fully. After spending the night in the hotel room Ryan had rented, he had told her he loved her and that she was his forever, and Carly had believed him. That last summer with him felt like life couldn't get any better. Up until the day he had to leave for his out-of-state college, she had no clue he was going to dump her. They had even slept together the morning of the day he broke up with her. Carly's heart burned with rage as she remembered how he had used her. He had lied, and manipulated her to get what he wanted and then threw her away like trash when he thought he could get someone better at college.

As Carly looked at Kyle laughing with their mixed group of friends, she felt certain that he was different from Ryan. She wasn't sure she was ready to give her heart away, but why not take a leap of faith and just try?

When Kyle set up an elaborate way to ask her out on a date that involved a dozen red roses, a large poster board and the entire football team participating, she felt like saying no would be too cruel. Besides, she liked Kyle and wanted to give him a shot.

Their date was going really well. Despite being February, the weather that day was warm and mild. Kyle took her to a restaurant across the street from the beach and had even packed a picnic dessert basket for them to enjoy at a secluded spot on the beach at sunset.

After dinner, they slid off their shoes and walked to a secluded spot on the beach. As they sat down on the blanket Kyle laid out for them, Carly pulled her sweater a little tighter to shield her from the cool afternoon ocean breeze. Kyle scooched closer and put an arm around her.

"That better?" he asked inches away from her face.

When he leaned in for a kiss, she put her hand on his muscular chest to tell him she wasn't ready to kiss anyone yet, but he grabbed her by her shoulders even more forcefully as he planted his mouth on hers. Within a split second he was laying on top of her trying to put his hand up her skirt. Carly's shock and horror helped her leap into action. She screamed at Kyle to stop.

"Get off me!"

She used her one free hand to repeatedly slap him. And then she used all her bodily force to kick up and push him off of her.

As she gained her bodily freedom she yelled, "What the hell are you doing!?" She was still shaking with fear and rage.

"What am I doing? What are you doing? Don't act all virtuous and prim. I've seen all your videos with Ryan. Besides, everyone knows Ryan only dates one kind of girl. The fact that he dated you for so long and all those videos he posted have most of the guys at our school fantasizing about being with you." Kyle was about to grab her for a second attack.

Carly stood up abruptly and took a few steps away. Panting for breath, she was horrified and shocked that all of the attention she has been eating up for the past five months was because these dumb idiots thought of her as nothing more than an object for their pleasure. Her mind was reeling.

"What videos?" Carly barely whispered as dread was growing in her stomach.

"Your videos. The ones you made with Ryan." Kyle growled. His eyes looked over her body leaving her in little doubt of the content of the videos he was talking about.

Carly's mind reeled. She had never made any videos and she couldn't understand what Kyle was talking about. Her brain felt like mush and her vision began to go narrow. She thought back to all the times she and Ryan had been together. He had been pretty particular about where they did the deed. But she had trusted him and loved him, never in her wildest imagining could she see Ryan filming her and then sharing those intimate videos with the world online. She thought he loved her and despite the situation she found herself in, she couldn't believe even now, that Ryan had secretly filmed her and posted her on the internet.

"You only asked me out because you thought I would sleep with you on the first date?" Her tone was a mix of despair and hate.

"I could have any girl I wanted at school. There's only one thing you're good for, Carly. I've paid good money to buy Ryan's videos of you. You owe me." Kyle justified.

Carly's jaw dropped. "Owe you for what? I never made any videos!" Carly screamed in hysteria. "You never paid me for anything." Carly felt like she couldn't breathe. The bomb that Kyle had dropped on her was enough to make her pass out, but she needed to get to safety first. She willed herself to keep fighting for consciousness. Keep breathing.

Carly picked up her purse, grabbed her sandals and started walking toward the bus stop. Her world had just imploded on her and she didn't want to give Kyle the satisfaction of knowing he had done worse than what he intended. This was a wound she didn't think she would ever recover from. Luckily, the bus pulled up within a few minutes of Carly crying at the bus stop. Luckily, Kyle was too big of a jerk to even bother chasing after her.

By the time Carly had walked down the street to her house, her tears had subsided. When Carly got home, she vaguely heard the concern in her mother's voice as she asked Carly, "What happened? Why did you walk home? Where's Kyle? Are you OK?" Shock was evident on her mother, Heidi's face.

Carly felt numb all over and even though her mother was now crying and asking all manner of questions, it felt as though it was some other person who was in the room. Carly felt as though she wasn't really in her own body anymore.

After Carly collapsed on her bed and slept for a while, she awoke to the nightmare she wished she had only dreamed. It was 11 p.m., but she called Ryan anyway. It was Friday and she doubted he would be asleep already.

"Hey Carly, I can't..." Ryan's voice was cut off by a voice Carly barely recognized.

"Did you video our intimate times together and sell it on the internet?" she asked calmly as if she were asking him how the weather was.

There was a long silence before Ryan let out his breath and said, "How do you think I could afford this college? My parents weren't going to help me and I didn't want to end school with a mountain of debt. I found a way and I took it. Listen, I gotta go. Don't call me again. I am changing my number." Ryan hung up.

Carly knew she should be hysterical. She knew she should be filled with all sorts of emotions, but she just felt dead inside: like she would never be able to feel anything ever again. She sent him a text. *"What's the website?"*

A few minutes later, Ryan texted her the web address. Carly clicked on the link and to her horror, there were over twenty videos of her and Ryan. He had thousands of subscribers. Hundreds of thousands of people she had never met, saw her lose her virginity to him. She hit play on the only free video and watched what she had once thought was a loving exchange. Carly noticed that the view of the camera was coming from what she remembered was a smoke alarm over the bed. She also noticed that the camera angle changed a few times. Clearly, Ryan must have had several hidden cameras set up in the room and either he or someone else had edited all the angles together to create what she was now watching.

Carly leaned over and vomited into her trash can. As she wiped a shaky hand across her mouth, she noticed that all of the girls Ryan had dated in the past two years were on this website with him. She had not been the first, and she knew she probably wouldn't be the last.

The next week, Carly didn't want to go to school. How could she face sitting next to Kyle Belfi after the little she had watched, and the numerous other videos he had admitted to paying for? She had tried to convince her mom that she needed to switch schools, but without coming clean and telling her mom everything that had happened there was no way to convince her to let her switch mid-year.

She wore her sweatpants and sweatshirt to school that whole week. Her mom, Heidi, had asked her why she was wearing the same thing each day, but Carly couldn't bring herself to talk about what had happened. The first day back Carly learned that Kyle had gotten his revenge on her slapping and refusing him by telling his football buddies that Ryan must have used up all the goods because she wasn't worth the price of a dinner date. He told everyone that would listen that she slept with him and wasn't any good. He degraded her to a worthless object, and what was worse was that everyone seemed to just take him at his word. No one seemed to question him and when her friends asked her about it, all she could say was that Kyle was a liar and a pervert. Carly became so altered from the experience that most people didn't believe her. Girls called her horrible names in the bathroom and hallways. Boys constantly asked if she would perform lewd acts on them in various gross school locations.

Within the span of a week, Carly had gone from being the most sought-after girl in school and enjoying all of the attention guys gave her, to wearing the baggiest, thickest clothes she had in her closet despite the warming weather, and secretly cutting her arms in an attempt to try and release her pain and misery.

By April, her locker had *"Slut"* painted on it with red nail polish and her Honda Accord had something similar etched into the driver's door. Girls seemed to think that she was sleeping with their boyfriends and they hated her no matter how she tried to deny it.

When the summer rolled around, Heidi had had enough of her "moping" and sent her to spend a few weeks with her dad and his wife, Shellie. Carly couldn't bear the pain of betrayal, the fear that everyone around her had seen her in vulnerable moments, and the anger burning in her stomach at what Ryan had done to her and what Kyle had said about her. As she made small slices into her arms, she gave into the misery and felt that the only way to truly end her pain was to end her life.

Carly ran the razor along the blue-green veins and hoped she would die quickly. When Shellie came barging into the bathroom to put folded towels away seconds after she had cut her wrists, Carly feared she might not have the ending she craved.

Chapter 1: Senior Year

Carly stood in the student parking lot, feeling her stomach churn with apprehension. Senior year was finally here, but she dreaded that Kyle's lies would somehow still haunt her even though he had graduated already. Carly worried that her past would never be forgotten and that no matter how small she made herself or how hard she tried to be invisible, those videos and rumors would be back to cause trouble for her. Or worse, some new guy would decide she made the perfect target and "pull a Kyle."

She looked at herself in the rearview mirror and said her mantra that the therapist from the psych ward had helped her create over the summer.

"Just keep your head down. It doesn't matter what other people believe; you know the truth. You are stronger than their lies."

She took in a deep breath in the hopes that it would settle her stomach before she grabbed her backpack off the passenger seat, slung it over her right shoulder, and opened her door just as the warning bell for first period rang out. She had exactly six minutes to get to her first class to avoid being marked tardy.

As she hurried along the path between the basketball courts and the football stadium, she pulled her hoodie up and put on her headphones. She hit play on her phone and Alanis Morisette's voice from her *Jagged Little Pill* album came on just in time to drown out the possibility of her hearing the taunts or greetings from anyone around her. Carly had started this routine last year after she went on that horrible date with Kyle. After which, Kyle started a bunch of rumors to get back at her for not wanting to sleep with him on their first date. Carly hated what a creep Kyle was and that she was stupid enough to fall for his charm long enough to agree to a date in the first place. She hated that her friends had to even ask her if the rumors were true. She hated that some of them chose to believe Kyle even after she told them what actually happened. She spent three months of her junior year eating lunch in a bathroom stall and wearing oversized hoodies no matter how hot they felt at the end of the year, just so she could avoid the harassing comments that Kyle and his buddies would make about her body. She hated everyone at this stupid school and she hated that she needed to finish high school in order to get out of this dumb town.

Carly turned her music up so loud that anyone walking near her could have also heard Alanis' voice ring out the lyric "What a jagged little pill." But no one was close enough to her for that. After her reputation at school was ruined, Carly had gotten good at pushing everyone away.

She had made it to her homeroom with Mr. Rodriquez in R-15 just as the final bell for class rang out. Carly had pushed pause on her music and was hastily putting her earphones away.

"Sit down please," Mr. Rodriguez said.

Carly made her way to an empty chair in the back of the room and threw her backpack down next to it before realizing Jill Goodmen was sitting right next to her. *Too late now,* she thought to herself as she sat down and tried to pretend she didn't see Jill sitting two feet away. Carly had refused to speak to Jill ever since she told her about what happened with Kyle, and Jill had made the comment that most rumors have an ounce of truth. After that, Carly had ghosted Jill. She never confronted her like she had with Darcy, she just chose not to speak to her anymore.

"Hey Carly," came Jill's bright cheerful voice.

Great. No choice now, Carly thought.

"Oh, hey Jill," Carly winced inside as she heard her own fake cheerful tone.

"Darcy and I were just talking about you last night and we were hoping one of us would have class with you before lunch. We eat at the benches next to the quad now. You can't even hear or see any of the dumb jocks that sit at the tables by the center tree in the quad any more. So, maybe you will come and hang out with us at lunch again?" Jill's eyes looked into Carly's questioningly.

"Oh. Wow. Uhm, well, wow. That is such a sweet offer, but I will have to give it some thought. I usually get a lot of work done at lunch so that I don't take any homework home. I work every night these days." Carly hoped Jill wouldn't see right through her lies, or at least wouldn't call her on them.

"I understand," Jill said as she looked down.

Carly thought she saw sadness when Jill turned away.

The rest of Carly's classes went by in their usual uneventful way. Class syllabi were handed out, and teachers gave stern warnings about cheating and being late to class. When the bell rang for lunch, Carly felt curious to see if Jill and Darcy were actually far enough away from Kyle's old gang of friends to make it a possible lunch spot for her too.

"Carly, wait up!" She heard someone say.

When she turned around, she saw Min's smiling circular face. Min was their class president, the most likely candidate for the valedictorian, and had been her best friend their freshman year of high school.

She had lost touch with Min long before she had started hiding in the bathroom to avoid the tormenting rumors and taunts that Kyle's lies had instigated.

"Min!" Carly said with genuine excitement as she waited for her shorter friend. When Min finally caught up to Carly the two girls embraced in a rocking hug.

"I was just on my way to find Darcy and Jill at the benches for lunch. Wanna come?" Carly asked with a lightheartedness she didn't feel.

"I usually eat sneakily in the library or the student council room during lunch, but since it's the first day, why not?" Min gave Carly one of her large winning smiles and linked arms with her as the two of them walked through the throng of boisterous students to the other side of the quad where the benches were.

When they arrived at the benches, Jill and Darcy were nowhere to be found. Suddenly, Carly was very thankful that she had bumped into Min and that she at least had one friend to chat with while she started eating her packed lunch sandwich. It was a full ten minutes before Darcy and Jill showed up with their cafeteria trays filled with soggy pizza-esque main courses and waxy bright red apples.

"Carly you came!" said Jill excitedly. "I didn't know if you would join us or I would have waited a few minutes before grabbing this oh-so-delicious meal." She gave her pizza a dubious poke.

Darcy set her tray down on the bench and went to give Carly a hug. "Gosh, it feels like I haven't seen you in forever!" Darcy said as she let Carly go.

Darcy and Carly lived ten houses away from each other on Coben Street and had spent a lot of time together at the beach in the past two weeks.

"Darc, I just saw you yesterday!" Carly said with a fake laugh. She couldn't tell if she was anxious or excited to be eating lunch with friends rather than sulking alone in her usual stinky hiding place.

"Oh I know, I just meant that it's been too long since I have gotten to hang with you at lunch time, at school." She jerked her chin in the direction of the center tree in the quad: the direction where Kyle used to eat lunch. "It has been too long since we last ate lunch together," Darcy said meaningfully.

Carly knew exactly what Darcy was referring to. The last time they ate lunch together, a baseball player named Zack had come up and asked her for a quickie in the boys' bathroom. She told him off like the pervy creep he was, but he said Kyle had told him she said "yes" to anyone: that she was easy. That was the day she learned just how Kyle got revenge on her for their confrontation on their one and only date.

The four girls settled into easy conversation about their class schedules, teachers, the friends they had class with and what they did over the summer.

Carly couldn't help but remember that the last time she and Jill had eaten lunch together, Jill had said "Well all rumors usually have an ounce of truth, I'm not judging you Carly I just want to know what the truth is so I can defend you."

Carly had wanted to slap Jill across her obnoxiously cheerful face, but instead she retorted in a deep, angry voice "this rumor doesn't have even an ounce of truth. Kyle thought he could force himself on me and when I fought back, he decided to lie about me. End of story!"

She had refused to eat lunch with her after that day and had sat on the back of a toilet and hid in a bathroom stall during lunch for the rest of the year. It was the only place at school where she didn't have to deal with other people and their mean comments.

All of these thoughts were racing in Carly's mind. She noticed that her heart was pounding and she felt sick to her stomach. It took everything in her to not leave and to try and remember that despite Jill's hurtful comment to her, she had in fact been her biggest defender. Jill had actually reported Kyle to the principal for bullying and sexual harassment. It went nowhere of course since Carly couldn't bring herself to face him in a meeting with the principal and their parents. But Jill had fought for her, and she had to cling to that memory instead of the one where she doubted her word.

Carly took a sip from her water bottle to steady herself as her friends chatted easily about how lame their classes were, or how they didn't get to sit near their friends, or how they couldn't wait for the homecoming dance. Carly sat on the bench doing her best to appear busy chewing so she didn't have to offer up much to the conversation. She forced herself to chuckle when they did and she tried to keep her mind focused on the present. Her eyes would wander to the top of the center tree and her mind would wander back to the bus ride home. To sobbing uncontrollably the entire trip back to her neighborhood. To trying to sneak into her house so that her mom wouldn't hear and wouldn't ask questions. To burning the outfit she had purchased and worn for her date in an aluminum trash can in the backyard. She found that it was this lighthearted chatter and silly jokes about oddly dressed teachers, classmates, and possible dates to the dance that kept her from being engulfed in her own despair.

The bell rang to signal the end of lunch. She had six minutes to get to her next class. She looked up at Jill who was just then slinging her messenger backpack over her shoulder and realized how good it felt to eat lunch with friends. Carly smiled at her little circle of friends and they smiled back.

Darcy gave Carly a quick hug. "If I don't start running now, I will never get to the Z building on time. I wish they would give us longer to get to our classes but Mr. Sims is a stickler and he will lock his door if you aren't inside when the bell rings. Carly, can you meet me here after school?" As soon as Carly had nodded, Darcy took off jogging toward the baseball fields and the string of trailers that served as the "Z buildings"

Min and Carly both had trigonometry in the E building which also took a full five minutes to walk to.

"See ya later Jill. Thanks for asking me to join you for lunch. It has been a breath of fresh air. Literally." Jill and Carly smiled in a knowing way.

On the way to their next class, Min shared with Carly that Kyle had dated Sara O. during the summer break and that Sara had dumped him after like a month. Sara was now best friends with the cheer captain, Lindsay who had told Min that Kyle had been a terrible boyfriend.

Carly did her best to encourage Min's communication without seeming overly interested.

Min said, "You can thank Sara for shutting up the whole football team about their love lives!"

"Really?" Carly asked

Min leaned in a little closer as she said, "Sara told Lindsay, who has basically told everyone she knows, that Kyle was a terrible lover..." Min wiggled her eyebrows in a meaningful way and then continued.

"She said that anyone who was friends with him was probably just as bad as him! She said Kyle was a big fat liar about everything, and anyone who was friends with him was probably a total liar too. Apparently, his old friends would rather throw him under the bus and distance themselves from him, than have their manly reputations questioned." Min gave a mocking laugh at their hypocrisy.

Carly had been scared that this new school year would be just as miserable as the last, but this bit of gossip from Min made her feel relieved. It seemed that a lot of the guys who had harassed her for months had moved on and she could handle the few vulgar jokes that a couple guys chose to yell at her. Besides, with her habit of keeping her earphones in, she barely even noticed them anymore.

Carly's last class of the day was government. She saw that she sat in front of Sara O. As Carly began walking out of class to meet up with Darcy in the Quad, she found that Sara was waiting for her.

"Carly, can I have a minute?" Sara asked.

"I gotta hurry to meet up with a friend. Can you walk with me?" Carly replied.

"Sure. I only need a minute," Sara said.

As they began walking, Carly noticed that Sara looked around. It seemed as if she was ensuring that no one she knew was close enough to overhear what she had wanted to tell Carly.

"I wanted to say that I am sorry for painting 'Slut' on your locker last year." Sara blurted out.

Carly had suspected a handful of girls who may have been responsible for the graffiti, but she had never suspected Sara.

"My friend Tracy's boyfriend had been bragging to all of his buddies that he was going to bang you behind the bleachers after school and Tracy was a wreck as you can imagine. She wasn't ready to sleep with Cole yet, and the fact that you were going to ruin everything made me boil. I know now that it wasn't actually true."

Carly raised an eyebrow as if to ask, *how do you suddenly know the truth?*

"I saw a video on Kyle's computer. Well, enough of it to know that he was obsessed with you. When I confronted Kyle about it and asked him if he had actually slept with you or just watched videos of you, he fessed up and told me it was all just a prank that had gotten out of hand."

Sara looked at Carly whose mouth was agape.

"I know! Like what kind of loser does that as a prank!? So anyways, I just wanted to come clean and tell you I'm sorry. I can't imagine how awful last year was for you dealing with the outrageous lies the guys were spreading, and I'm sorry I added to the drama."

Sara looked down and put her hand to her chest. "Wow, my therapist was right. I do feel a lot better with that off my chest." Sara gave a soft laugh before she said, "K. well that's all I needed to say. I hope you won't hold it against me." She checked her phone for the time. 'Yikes, I gotta go and get ready for cheer practice. Bye!"

Carly couldn't believe what she had heard. She knew the football team had been tormenting her with their comments, but she hadn't known just how bad things really were. She had seen that Sara looked genuinely sorry, but was glad she was spared from needing to actually reply to her. Sara was not someone she felt she could trust, and Carly was thankful she was too self-absorbed to require a response. Carly also wasn't sure if she could ever forgive her for the torment her actions had caused her those last few weeks of school.

Carly walked deep in thought to the quad to meet up with Darcy.

Darcy had just pulled her day planner out of her backpack when Carly walked up.

"I wasn't sure how long you were going to be so I thought I would work on my homework calendar while I waited," Darcy said lightly as she got up and gathered her things.

"Hey, my mom has let me start driving my car again, so we don't have to take the bus or walk," Carly said sheepishly.

"What! Why didn't you tell me yesterday when I called you? That's great news! We are going to be driving home in style!" Darcy exclaimed.

"Thanks Darc. She just surprised me this morning with my keys. I guess she figured I was recovered enough to handle the pain of driving a car with a curse word etched into the door. Plus, she knows I would rather skip school than take the bus ever again." Carly had skipped ten days of school the previous year before her mom had started driving her to ensure she went. When she got her license and her own car at the end of the school year, she felt relief, but after her stint in the psych ward, her mom had taken her car away and told her she would only get it back when she felt she was ready for it. Carly had worked hard to convince her mom she was fine by working with her at her cleaning company and doing everything she could to seem normal.

"You didn't get rid of the profanity?" Darcy said skeptically.

"Nope, someone's jealous girlfriend worked hard to adorn my door with a word that rhymes with witch," Carly said as humorously as she could muster.

Darcy's expression was a mix of anger and sadness. "Is there any way you could paint over it or something?" she asked hopefully.

"I am sure there is, I just haven't had any money to put into it. Gas and insurance take up most of my paycheck and I put the rest into savings so that I can hopefully afford to attend college and buy books," Carly said as she started walking toward the parking lot. She knew Darcy would follow after her and she didn't want to keep talking about the painful things that happened last year, especially not in the quad where every spot was triggering bad memories for her.

The drive home was pleasant. Darcy didn't bother making Carly catch up on all the things she missed while hiding from the shame of the rumors. She just turned on her favorite Counting Crows CD and they rolled the windows down while they sang badly at the top of their lungs. It felt like old times to Carly, like before her world had been dowsed with pain and misery.

Chapter 2: How They See Her

The first week of school went by in a fast blur. Carly had forgotten how sweet a few good friends could make life. When the drama with Kyle broke out, she was so embarrassed and ashamed that she hid herself away from everyone. She couldn't take the looks, the comments, the snickering in her direction, or worse the pitying "You, OK?" her friends repeatedly said with their concerned looks.

Senior year was going to be so much better than her junior year. She just knew it.

As Carly walked into the kitchen to grab a cup of coffee and make some toast for breakfast before she set off for school, she found that her mother was sitting at her tiny desk in the corner of their kitchen working on her laptop surrounded by several stacks of papers.

"Carly, don't forget. You are starting back at work with me tonight. I want to have a few days of us working together before I leave you in charge of your crew," Heidi said in the brisk tone she always assumed when she talked about work.

"Yes, Mom. I know," Carly said while rolling her eyes at the cup of coffee she was stirring cream into. She had learned early on in life that it never paid to show her irritation or anger with her mom. It only brought her more frustration.

"Jessica has said that she will help you manage the team if they give you any grief. You know how important this is to growing the business," Heidi said with a stern look on her face.

It bothered Carly that her mom still didn't think she could run a crew by herself. She had been unofficially working in her mom's cleaning business since the beginning when she was five. She had more knowledge and experience than most of the older women on her crew and she knew how to get the work done quickly and keep everyone on task.

"Mom, I know what I am doing! You don't need to put Jessica on my crew to babysit me!" Carly insisted.

"I know darling, but it will make me feel better knowing that Jessica is with you. She is the best I have aside from you and I plan to give her a crew soon too. I just need to hire a few more women after I secure the new office cleaning contracts," Heidi said soothingly as she began shuffling through a stack of papers.

Heidi's cleaning business was an all-female company. She had repeatedly told Carly over the years that "I made the mistake of trusting a man once in my life and all that got me was pregnant and miserable." Carly knew Heidi loved her, but she also knew all too well that Heidi regretted getting pregnant when she was nineteen. When her father, Nick, left her mom, she was only four years old and Heidi began working as a cleaning lady to try and support the two of them. Nick had divorced her mom because he said he didn't need all her "drama" as he had called it. Carly knew her mom had always resented Nick for first getting her pregnant and then abandoning her because she was constantly angry with him for flirting with other women and not being around enough. Heidi had worked hard over the past thirteen years to grow her business, and she was closer than ever to reaching her goal of being able to focus solely on the business side of things and stop being one of the cleaners. Heidi poured her heart and soul into her cleaning company as if success in her work would remove all of the wounds and disappointments of the past.

"How long are you going to leave Jessica in my crew?" Carly questioned as she took a sip of her coffee.

"Just until I have enough women trained for her to start her own crew. I also am waiting for my bids on the new office buildings to be accepted so that there is enough business to support the expanding crews," Heidi said as she began typing information from one of the papers into her laptop.

Carly was well aware that her mom had recently bid on ten different cleaning contracts for office suites in their area and was feeling confident that at least three of them would be accepted. Heidi had made sure that her prices were competitive while still being profitable. As Heidi became fully absorbed in her work, Carly knew she had better get to school and leave her alone. Her mom hated being interrupted while she was working.

***

"Uh, earth to Carly!" Darcy said as they were pulling up tó school. "Girl, where did you go?" I was telling you about the Eco club and the volunteer opportunities and you just went all blank and stopped responding!"

"Oh, I'm sorry. I guess I was just zoning out. I have to start working nights again today and I have a mountain of homework and then the thought of having to do volunteer work to look good on college applications just felt overwhelming. It's not fair. Work experience should be enough for colleges. Why do I have to volunteer too?" Carly felt frazzled as the words flooded out of her mouth.

"Don't look at me," Darcy stated as she threw her hands up as if she were saying she did not have all the answers. "I just repeat what my guidance counselor and parents tell me."

Both of Darcy's parents were college graduates. Her dad had a Master's in Business and her mom had a Bachelor's in Finance. Her family was what Carly used to dream of hers being. Carly had thought that when her dad, Nick, had finally asked her to move in with him and his new wife, Shellie, that she would have the family she dreamed of. She should have known they only wanted her to babysit her newborn brother, Joey, while they went out living their best life. She should have known that her dad only loved himself. Shellie tried to love Carly and take care of her, but she was only thirteen years older than her, and they always felt more like sisters, than a daughter and a step-mother. When Ryan had dumped her so he could enjoy his college experience, she had tried to get love and sympathy from her dad, but there was none.

"Mija what did you expect? Huh?" Carly's dad, Nick, said. His Mexican-Spanish accent was always more prominent when he was trying to be soothing and tender. "Ryan is a good-looking guy and of course he wants to date other girls when he goes to college. High school is supposed to be fun, huh? He was good to you while it lasted. Why are you so upset?"

Carly could see that her dad was genuinely confused why anyone would bother with being sad over a relationship ending. But he had never been dumped though. He always moved on to a new woman before he ended the relationship with the former, so it made sense that he would see Ryan as a "good guy." After that encounter, Carly had asked her mom if she could work for her full-time and get a raise. Heidi wasn't thrilled at the prospect, but Carly had promised to work hard and not complain. Carly had thrown herself into work to avoid the ache of heartbreak.

Carly's heart craved the kind of love that Darcy's family seemed to have for each other. Her parents had been married for twenty-two years and they still liked each other. But Carly knew that no matter how much she dreamed of being a part of a loving family like Darcy's, she could never have that.

"...So pick me up on Saturday at 8 a.m. and I'll pay for our coffee before we spend the whole day cleaning the beach," Darcy said while she wrote their plans down in her new school day planner.

"8 a.m. is too early! What time do we have to be there? You know I work Friday nights until 11 p.m." Carly whined.

"Girl, weren't you listening to anything I just said?" Darcy gave Carly a worried look. "The beach clean up day starts at 9 a.m. and you have to get there ten minutes early to sign in and have them sign your volunteer hours, otherwise you're just doing it to be a good person," Darcy quickly summed up.

"Oh right. OK. Well, I guess if we stop for coffee, I can make it work," Carly said as she put her car in park and they got out of it in time to hear the first warning bell.

"I'll buy you the largest coffee and a bagel. Don't look so gloomy. It's going to be fun! I'm so glad you are coming with me." Darcy smiled broadly as she half-yelled the last sentence because she had already began walking to her class.

"If you say so." Carly shrugged as she too started walking quickly towards her homeroom.

School went by like an uneventful breeze. Carly was enjoying the reprieve from the harassment of the football team and their followers thanks to the backlash Sara O. had instigated during the summer and first week of school. Carly enjoyed walking the hallways and eating in public without being subjected to disgusting comments or suggestions.

Later that evening, she got ready for her first shift as a crew leader. She felt like a fraud because she wasn't actually going to be leading anyone this week. Her mom didn't know how to be anything other than the boss. Even when her mom wasn't there, Jessica would be, and since Jessica was a thirty-three-year-old grown woman, it made it hard for the other women, who were also all older than Carly, to take her authority seriously. She did her makeup to try and give her a few extra years. She slicked her hair back like her mom's and hoped it was enough to make her look the part.

As the days went by, Carly found that cleaning the offices was going better than she had anticipated. The other women on her crew respected her leadership, and true to her word, Heidi had only worked with Carly for the first three days before leaving her in charge. Even Jessica was working hard to support her authority and hadn't stepped out of line once. Carly found that she was more confident in her new role than she had imagined she would feel. She had even stopped wearing makeup to look older which she discovered was impractical anyway. She was excited that she could finally delegate the tasks she hated, specifically cleaning the bathrooms. She would wipe windows and counters, vacuum and empty trashcans all by herself if it meant she didn't have to go anywhere near the toilets. Eventually, this became her crew's routine. They would all start cleaning the windows together and then the three other women would go clean the two five-stall bathrooms while Carly took care of the rest.

One night while her crew were all cleaning the two large bathrooms, Carly worked quietly and quickly to get the other tasks done. As she entered into one of the private offices to empty the trash and vacuum, Carly was startled to see a handsome young man busy working at the desk.

"Oh, I'm so sorry to interrupt. Is it alright if I vacuum in here or would you prefer that I skip this room tonight?" Carly asked politely.

The young man looked bewildered by her presence, as if he had been staring at the computer screen for so long, that he had lost all track of time. He looked at his watch and then said, "I didn't realize it had gotten so late. Uh, I will be done in a few minutes. Why don't you skip this office for now and come back then?" His tone seemed to be asking rather than telling.

"Yes, Sir," Carly replied simply and turned to leave the room. She didn't want him to see the color rising to her face. He was so good looking and Carly had been almost stunned at finding a handsome young man. She felt sure if she didn't leave quickly, he would know how embarrassed she was at being seen in her oversized neon pink work shirt and without any makeup on. When Carly came back to the office later that night, the young man was nowhere to be found but on his desk was a note that read,

"To the cleaning staff,

Thank you for waiting for me to finish cleaning this office. I appreciate your courtesy. -Daniel Morse"

Daniel Morse is a hottie, Carly thought to herself and then she looked quickly around to make sure no one else caught her awkwardly hugging the note she just read. She placed the note back down quickly on the desk, finished cleaning, and left for the night wondering if she would ever see Daniel again.

The next night Carly made sure she had her makeup on and that her hair was a little more flattering than a slicked-back tight bun. She told herself she was just trying to look more professional and put together, but in her innermost heart, she wondered if she was hoping to look more attractive just in case she ran into the handsome young business man again.

Carly shook her head at her own stupidity when she went into the same private office that Daniel was at, and he wasn't there. Carly knew that her mom intentionally started their cleaning shift two hours after the office buildings closed for business so that they didn't have to worry about disruptions from people working late. But despite her logic, her heart felt as though it had dropped into her stomach at her secret disappointment of not finding him there again.

After a week of wearing makeup and styling her hair for work, Carly finally gave up hope of seeing Daniel again. She went back to her makeup-less, slicked-back bun look because it was more practical after all. Cleaning multiple offices as quickly as possible always made her sweaty and wearing makeup while she sweat inevitably led to breakouts. As she made her way to the back office, she noticed the light was still on. She groaned inside, *Oh of all the days! Of course, this would be the one he is here! When I look terrible and have a huge zit in between my eyebrows.* Carly was dreading seeing Daniel again but when she went into the office, no one was there. *It was just a light left on.* She sighed in relief to herself.

Just as she was finishing up in the back office, and was heading out the door, she looked up to see Daniel holding a mug walking toward her.

Carly abruptly lowered her head and stepped out of his way. She knew her movements were hasty and awkward so she pulled out a rag from her back pocket and began wiping down the hallway wall as if she was just trying to wipe some dirt smudges off.

"Hello again," Daniel's smooth masculine voice said.

"Oh... hello sir," Carly said sheepishly. She had been hoping he wouldn't recognize her.

"Sir?" he questioned. "I guess in these clothes I seem much older." He paused as if waiting for a response, but Carly just kept scrubbing away at the already-clean wall hoping he would move on soon.

"My father runs this company and is trying to get me started down the same career path. I'm lucky to have such a great position, but because we are family, he hounds me the hardest. That's why I have to work late so often." His eyes were locked on Carly.

Carly looked up from wiping down an imaginary scuff off the hallway wall as he spoke. His voice seemed tired yet determined. But she found herself wondering, "Why are you telling me all this?"

She was surprised when she realized she had said it out loud.

"I guess I just wanted you to know that I wasn't an old 'sir' and I also wanted to talk to you. How old are you, ma'am?" he said playfully.

For a moment Carly deliberated if she should tell him her age. He seemed handsome and charming, but once he found out that she was still seventeen he would probably want nothing to do with her.

"I am almost eighteen," she finally admitted.

"Well, I am almost twenty-three," he replied with a smile. "Hardly old enough for you to call 'sir.'"

Carly found herself smiling back at him just as her crew came into the room to finish their nightly routine.

Upon seeing her crew, Carly stumbled away from his office in embarrassment and said, "I have to finish my work. Good night." She turned hastily away from Daniel and went quickly to her crew.

To her amazement, none of the women in her crew said anything or made any jokes about finding her chatting with a handsome guy in the hallway when she was supposed to be cleaning. Not until they were all safely in the parking lot putting the supplies away in the van.

"Who was that cutie?" Belinda, a member of the cleaning crew asked.

"Cutie?" Jessica laughed. "More like who was that stud?"

"He's just some guy that works there. He said he has to work late often because his dad runs the company and has higher standards for him than the rest of the employees." Carly hoped she had sounded more casual and disinterested than she really felt.

The other women all started laughing and giving their silliest impressions of Daniel. "Ooo. Look at me. I'm a tall good-looking boss' son," Rose said in a silly deep voice. Carly wanted to cry but did her best to laugh with the others so as not to show how she was affected.

"OK, we are all done here. I'm tired and want to go home. See you tomorrow," Carly said curtly as she got into the van to start driving away.

The other women in her crew all sauntered off to their own vehicles. Some were singing love songs and sashaying down to the cars, others were laughing too hard to look anything more than silly. Carly was just glad she could go home and get away from everyone, except Jessica.

Jessica had been her mom's friend before Heidi had started her cleaning business, and so she always drove to their house and rode in the cleaning van with her to the job site. It was Heidi's request that two crew members were always in the van so that if anything happened, they were better equipped to deal with it.

As Carly pulled the van into the driveway and put it in park, Jessica looked cautiously at her and said, "Hey, in all seriousness, don't let yourself get involved with that man. He comes from a different world and he will bring you nothing but trouble. Best to date men who don't see you as the help." She undid her seatbelt and began to grab her bag.

Carly felt her anger rising. "Oh, so I should only date men who are equally as poor as me? Men whose best work options are to be garbage truck drivers, or construction workers? Just who exactly do you think is in the same class as me?" Carly said furiously.

"Oh sweetheart, I didn't mean it like that. I just know that once a business man thinks of you as the cleaning lady, they tend to think they are better than you and that you owe them something and it makes for trouble in relationships. I once dated a business man and let's just say, he didn't end up treating me well." Jessica pointed to a small scar above her eyebrow.

"Oh, I'm sorry," Carly mumbled. She felt torn. She wanted someone like Daniel to want to date her. He was old enough and different enough to pull her out of her world, but she also feared that maybe she was making too much of their two small encounters. Maybe there was nothing to hope for anyway. There was no point in arguing about it right now. Not when it was late, they were both tired, and Daniel had done nothing more than tell her about his job and age.

Carly left the van in a huff. She felt that life was utterly unfair. Other kids her age were out partying and living it up; they were enjoying their last year of high school, while she was slaving away at her mother's business just so she could try and save up enough money to get away from this horrible city where her life had been utterly ruined. She couldn't even date anyone from school because all the guys at school were too risky ever since she learned about the videos and Kyle had made sure to ruin her reputation. Now, she had finally met a handsome guy who knew nothing about her traumatic past, and he was off limits because he was too above her?! It was just her usual luck.

When Carly got into her room, she blasted her headphones. The music helped to mask the rage and ache in her heart, but it felt like nothing would ever make all the pain go away. She wanted a solution for the hurt, but the only one her mom knew was to just never let herself feel anything. Her dad literally never cared about anyone other than himself so he knew nothing of hurt. Darcy and Jill had happy, normal lives. They couldn't relate to the trauma she went through last year, and their sympathy made Carly's skin crawl. She hated feeling like everyone was just feeling sorry for her all of the time, and yet she didn't know how to make it all go away; to go back to the days when she was just a normal girl.

After lying in bed listening to her music so loudly she couldn't hear herself think for some time, Carly finally managed to fall asleep.

Chapter 3: The Beach Cleanup

At 7:30 a.m. on Saturday morning, Carly's alarm went off bright and early. *Why is my alarm ringing? It's too early,* Carly thought as she hit the snooze button, rolled over and went back to sleep only to be annoyingly woken up seven minutes later. Snooze! Carly didn't know how many times she had hit the snooze button before her phone started ringing.

"Ugh, I'm coming I'm coming!" She whined. Carly looked all over the floor to try and find the source of her ringing phone. She had forgotten to put it on her charger last night and it had fallen off her bed from all her tossing and turning. At last, she found it and hit the answer button.

"Carly, where are you? I've been knocking on your door for like four minutes, we won't have time for coffee if you don't hurry!" Darcy yelled.

Realization suddenly hit Carly and the adrenaline hit her body causing her to spring into action. She put some crumpled-up jeans on, a mostly clean shirt she had left on the end of her bed because she hadn't decided if it should go into the hamper yet, threw her hair into a ponytail, and ran to the door.

"I am so sorry!" she said breathlessly to Darcy. "I completely overslept."

Darcy looked like she already guessed as much. "If you want to get coffee, we have to leave in two minutes, otherwise we won't make it in time."

"Perfect. That is all I need!" Carly exclaimed as she whizzed off to the bathroom to brush her teeth and wash her face. She figured she could just bring some sunscreen and makeup to apply in the car while Darcy grabbed the coffee.

"All done," she said while throwing her makeup bag into her large purse.

By the time they got to the beach cleanup event, you would never have known that Carly had gotten ready in two minutes and that her makeup was done in the car. She was so naturally beautiful that she didn't really need the mascara, concealer, and lip tint anyway.

Carly and Darcy walked to the sign-up table to get their trash bags and trash grabbers when Carly suddenly froze.

"What's up?" Darcy asked.

"This is so embarrassing, but the guy at the table handing out the trash bags is someone I know from work!" Carly couldn't believe that Daniel of all people was working the beach cleanup event.

"He's cute!" Darcy said a little too loudly. Carly could swear that Daniel had heard Darcy's comment because he smiled ever so slightly after she said it.

As they neared the front of the volunteer line, Carly felt her heart start to pound. *What is this?* she thought. *Why am I nervous over some guy who barely knows me? He probably won't even recognize me out of my gross work outfit.*

"Hey! It is you," Daniel said with a cheerful smile. "What are the chances that I would run into you here?"

"I know right? Small world." Carly hoped she sounded casual and natural, despite feeling so awkward.

"OK, well let me finally get your name… So that I can get you signed in." Daniel seemed to add that second part like he had to justify asking for her name.

Carly smiled as she introduced herself and Darcy to Daniel.

So, he was trying to get to know me. The thought gave Carly pleasure. But then she worried that maybe somehow, he had seen her online and thought the same about her that all the guys at school seemed to think; that she was only good for one thing. Carly's stomach churned at the thought, and she had to force her thoughts back to the present moment to avoid having a panic attack.

As Carly and Darcy started to walk down the beach and pick up trash, Darcy looked surreptitiously back at Daniel and said, "How long have you been flirting with Hottie over there?"

Carly blushed and hastily turned to pick up some bits of plastic food wrappers out of the sand. She needed a moment to gather her thoughts.

"I've only known he exists for about a week or two. We ran into each other while I was working last night, but we were quickly interrupted by the rest of the crew coming in so we could finish cleaning and get home," Carly replied.

Darcy's eyebrows shot up in surprise. "You've had a mystery man fling for over a week and this is the first time I am finding out about it? Girl! I thought we were best friends." She sounded playfully indignant.

"It's nothing, Darc. He's just some guy."

Darcy looked dubious.

"Really! Nothing has happened. Last night was the first night I really even spoke to him. And as you just saw, he didn't even know my name. Also, I have been warned off of him. Jessica gave me an entire lecture last night on the way home about how I need to only date men in my economical class." Carly couldn't help rolling her eyes as she said this last part. She still hated the idea that Jessica felt someone like Daniel was too good for her.

"What a bunch of bull!" Darcy shouted.

Carly grew uncomfortable as other volunteers all looked in their direction. Darcy noticed that a lot of heads were turned in their direction so she quickly shouted, "Look at all this trash. Am I right or what? People who litter should be fined!"

After a moment of focusing on picking up trash, and allowing everyone else to stop looking at them, Darcy resumed.

"There. Now no one is looking at us, except the occasional glances from mystery-man over there." Darcy wiggled her eyebrows and made a kissy face at Carly.

"Can we just forget about Daniel and focus on the clean-up?" Carly begged.

"Sure girl, but you know the moment we get in the car I'm going to need about a million answers. Also, Jessica is not even remotely in the same "class" as you. She is ghetto to her core and doesn't aspire to be anything other than a caricature of a woman from some sleazy rap song. She has no business giving you advice!" Darcy said with passionate indignation.

Carly knew this was an unjust description of Jessica, but it felt so nice to be thought of as miles above her, to have her friend tell her she could date someone like Daniel, to be well thought of and loved, that she just smiled back and didn't correct Darcy.

The beach clean-up went by faster than Carly thought it would. By the end of the event, she was slightly sweaty, ravenously hungry, and ready to get out of there.

As Carly and Darcy made their way back to the check-in table to hand in their vests and trash pokers, Carly couldn't help but feel her stomach churn. Daniel was back at the table passing out bottles of water and collecting the volunteers' equipment.

Just as they got to the front of the table to lay their items down, Daniel rushed over to Carly.

"Hey, I only have a second, but I really wanted to invite you out to lunch. I'm done here in about ten minutes; would you mind waiting for me so I can take you out?" Daniel said.

Carly felt the heat rise to her face. "Oh. Uh, that is so sweet, but Darcy and I drove together, so that won't be possible today." She turned to look at Darcy but noticed Darcy had conveniently left to throw her empty water bottle away in the trashcan farthest from them.

She noticed Daniel seemed disappointed. "I can give you my number if you want to try for another time," she suggested and watched as his face transformed into a broad smile.

"Yes please! I would love that." Daniel pulled out his cell phone and asked Carly for her digits.

"I don't answer my phone often, so if I miss your call, please just leave a message," Carly said quickly. She hoped her embarrassment wasn't obvious. She could never bring herself to explain to him that the real reason she didn't answer her phone very often was because she had gotten so many harassing phone calls and explicit texts from guys at her school that she now got anxious when it rang with an unknown number.

"Yes ma'am," Daniel said, still grinning. Carly watched as Daniel punched in her number and then hit the call button. He got her voicemail message and said, "Hey Carly, this is Daniel, are you free for dinner tonight? I can pick you up at 7 p.m. or we can meet at any place you choose. Call me back."

He hung up the call, smiled, and said, "I have to finish up here, but I really would love to take you out and get to know you more."

"I don't have any plans for tonight so I guess when I get home, I will give you a call back and arrange the details." Carly smiled and walked away. She felt she needed to get home as soon as possible to have the most amount of time to get ready and hopefully look cute for her date.

As Carly headed toward her car, Darcy caught up with her and asked, "So??"

Carly couldn't help the big smile on her face as she said, "He asked me out! He wanted to go to lunch but I said no, so he got my number and asked me to dinner!"

Darcy gave a squeal of delight as she wiggled around in her happy dance.

When they got into the car, Darcy was asking questions at a mile a minute, but what they spent the majority of their time discussing was where Carly might go to dinner and what she should wear.

"Is he going to pick you up or do you plan on meeting him there?" Darcy asked.

"I will never ride with a guy for a first date," Carly said flatly. "I learned that lesson the hard way."

Darcy looked down as she said, "Right. Sorry."

"Besides, I don't want Daniel to know where I live. Jessica made it clear that he's in a different tax bracket than us, and I don't want him to look down on where I live," Carly said, trying to change the subject.

"Carly, our street is not a bad part of town," Darcy said defensively. "But I agree that stranger-man doesn't need your home address for a first date."

"I still can't believe I am going out on a date!" Carly said with a grin.

"Girl, if anyone deserves to have an incredible first date, it's you. I am praying this one is amazing," Darcy said.

Carly knew that Darcy liked to pray about everything, and even though she didn't believe in God, she liked the idea that her friend loved her enough to pray for her to her God.

When Carly got home, she mustered up the courage to call Daniel back.

"Hey Carly!" He answered on the first ring.

"Hi," she said sheepishly.

"So do you have any food allergies or preferences I should know about?" Daniel asked.

"Well, I don't really like seafood," Carly answered. "But I'm not allergic to anything.

"Great! I know of the perfect place. Can I pick you up at six?"

"No, I prefer to drive myself until I know you a lot better. I just feel better that way." Carly worried about how Daniel would respond.

"No problem. I get it. You don't know how safe and reliable I am yet," he said without missing a beat.

Carly could hear his smile through the phone.

"So where should I meet you?" Carly asked.

"I am taking you to the nicest restaurant I can think of. The steakhouse by the pier. Is that alright?" For the first time, Daniel sounded a little unsure of himself.

Carly was relieved to hear that the restaurant was outside of her city. She knew that anywhere near her home she was likely to run into people from her school and she had been dreading that possibility.

"Oh yeah, that's fine. I know the one you're talking about."

"Let's plan on meeting in the restaurant at 6:45 pm. I can't wait to see you then." Carly couldn't help but notice how manly and earnest Daniel's voice was.

"OK! See you then," Carly replied as she hung up.

Chapter 4: The Date

Carly looked at her clock, it read, 4:15 p.m. She had two hours to finish getting ready before she needed to drive over to the restaurant. Plenty of time to get dolled up and eat another bowl of cereal before she left for her date.

Her mother had taught her that it was unladylike to eat a large or heavy meal when on a date. Heidi had strict ideas about how a woman should behave on a date. Heidi herself only ever ordered a salad on the first two dates. She said you have to wait for the third date before you can order anything larger or kiss the guy.

Carly didn't want to take all of her mom's dating advice since Heidi had never had any serious relationships since her father, Nick. In fact, her relationships very rarely lasted longer than a couple of months.

Carly put on a pink floral spaghetti strap sundress that had sat in the back of her closet for the past few years with a pair of light blue wedge heels. She took care to do her makeup, so that it made her features pop, but still gave a natural look. Once she was ready and satisfied with her appearance, Carly grabbed a book to read and put it in her large bohemian purse. She was almost always early to everything and so reading in her car beforehand had become a customary practice for her.

"Bye Mom. I'll see you later tonight," Carly yelled from the living room as she dug through her purse for her keys.

"Wait. Hold on. Where are you going?" Heidi said confusedly.

Carly had wanted to avoid this conversation, but it looked like she had no choice but to confront her fears.

"I am going on a date. The guy working the volunteer table at the beach clean-up asked me out." It was all technically true. She just hadn't mentioned that it was the same guy she met at the offices she cleaned and who Jessica warned her never to date.

"Oh, how nice. Well, you look lovely." Heidi appraised Carly wearing a real dress and not an oversized t-shirt or sweatshirt and clearly was pleased that Carly had donned something other than her usual baggy armor.

"Where is he taking you, and when will you be home?" Heidi asked.

"We are meeting for dinner at the steakhouse on the pier and I don't know when I'll be home exactly, but I am guessing before 10 p.m. Can I go now?" It was fast approaching 6:17 p.m. and Carly was feeling anxious that she might actually be late for their first date.

"Yes honey, have a great time. Order a salad and remember, no kissing until the third date. You have to make men wait," Heidi reminded.

"Yes, Mom I know. I love you," Carly said as she gave her mom a quick kiss on her cheek.

"See you later," Heidi replied. And with that, Carly walked out the door.

When Carly arrived to the steak house it was 6:59 p.m. Traffic had been worse than she had thought and she hated that she was late for their first date. She parked her car close to the entrance in case she needed a quick getaway and decided to leave her book in her car. She didn't want to look too nerdy.

She walked into the entrance and immediately saw Daniel standing at the hostess' booth. He was dressed very nicely and was holding flowers. Carly felt like maybe she hadn't gotten dressed up enough for this date and instantly began wishing she had worn a fancier dress.

"There you are. Wow, you look amazing!" Daniel said as he came to stand near her.

Carly smiled up at him and replied, "You look pretty spiffy yourself!"

Daniel grinned and said, "The hostess says our table is just about ready." Daniel motioned for them to sit on one of the benches in the foyer to wait.

As Carly's eyes fell on the assorted bouquet of flowers in his hand he said, "Oh, these are for you," and handed her the bouquet.

Carly didn't have time to respond to the sweet gesture when the hostess cut in. "Daniel, your table is ready. If you will both follow me, I will take you to it."

They walked in silence to the table. When they got to their table Daniel insisted on holding out Carly's chair for her and scooting it in for her. She felt this was a little ridiculous, but she liked how hard he was trying to be courteous and charming.

"Have you ever been here before?" Daniel asked.

Carly didn't want to tell him that this place was way more expensive than the restaurants she normally went to but she also couldn't bring herself to lie to him just to impress him.

"Nope. I haven't. What's good here?" she replied.

"Honestly, I have only ever been here a couple of times for business meetings when we were trying to impress clients. We always ordered the steak and lobster dinner. But I don't actually like lobster. This was the nicest restaurant I could think of and well, I wanted to impress you." He laughed as he owned the truth about his experiences.

Carly blushed at his flattering admission. "Well consider me impressed," she said, giving her most winsome smile.

When it came time to order, Carly knew she would be getting the steak salad. It was cheap enough for her to afford it, but expensive enough that she hoped she didn't look cheap.

Daniel ordered a steak with mashed potatoes and green beans.

"So, tell me about yourself," he said after they handed the waitress their menus.

Carly knew she would have to tell him the truth if she wanted things to continue, so she took a sip of her water and said, "Well, I am a senior in high school. I work full-time as a lead cleaner for my mom's cleaning company, and I volunteer on occasion so that my college applications are as robust as possible." She hated having to own that she was still a high school student; it made her feel small.

"Whoa, you're in high school still! You seem so mature and sophisticated." The way Daniel looked her over sent a tingling sensation down Carly's spine before worry over his intentions set her guard up and made her anxious.

Daniel didn't seem to notice the effect he had on her and went on, "I am twenty-two, I graduated from the state university last year. I have been working for my dad's company ever since, and between you and me, he thinks I'm a moron because I often don't understand his backward approach to business." He took a drink of soda, and looked at Carly to see her reaction.

"Oh, so we both work in the family business. I think it's a parent's job to hound you and try to make you feel inferior in the workplace. It's like they think that if you survive their torture then you'll be even greater." Carly laughed. She had wanted to direct the conversation away from her age or anything that made her feel inadequate with this guy.

"I totally agree. So what colleges are you trying to apply to?"

Carly listed a few of the local colleges and then she listed a few out-of-state ones. Daniel was easy to talk to and seemed to know a great deal about several of her college choices.

When dinner arrived, Carly was pleased with her salad. It was finely chopped and the steak was thinly sliced. It would be easy to eat and still appear dignified. She laughed when Daniel shoved his napkin in his shirt collar as he prepared to eat his meal.

"What are you doing?" Carly asked with a chuckle.

"Oh this? Well, this is a standard fine dining practice. Didn't you know?" Daniel teased.

"But in all seriousness, I eat like a caveman and tend to drip on my shirt. And I would like to not look like a total slob when we leave this place." Daniel grinned at Carly as he reached for the bottle of steak sauce in the center of their table.

Carly loved how honest and open Daniel was. He was the perfect blend of open frankness while still showing all of the signs of wanting to impress her, even after she admitted she was still in high school.

When they were just about finished eating dinner, Daniel asked if she would be open to walking down the beach to the ice cream shop not very far off. Carly's anxiety and panic began to rise and she struggled to control her breathing. The last time she had gone on a date at the beach her world had collapsed around her. Carly didn't want her past to continue to haunt her, but the idea of walking on the beach with Daniel had already set her heart beating wildly and her stomach churning.

Daniel seemed to sense her apprehension and quickly added, "Or we could go up the boardwalk to the cupcake place."

"I would much prefer a cupcake I think," Carly admitted as calmly as she could muster. She was thankful he was so sensitive and seemed in tune with her.

When the bill came, Carly reached out to grab it and pay for at least her portion, but Daniel playfully yanked the bill out of her reach. "Um, I don't know what kind of dates you normally go on, but with me, you will not be allowed to pay for the meal." He winked.

Carly had mixed feelings. She loved that he wanted to take care of her and pay, but she dreaded it might mean he felt she was indebted to him and expect something from her.

"OK. Well at least let me pay for dessert or something," Carly bargained.

"I'm sorry, Miss Morales, but your request has been denied. We hope you understand," Daniel said with a playful smile.

As they got up to leave the restaurant, he looked down at Carly and said, "You still up for dessert?" He seemed unsure after their little quarrel over who got to pay.

"I suppose so," Carly said with a sweet smile.

"Great!" Daniel exclaimed and he opened the door to the restaurant for her to walk out

While they were walking down the boardwalk, He grabbed hold of Carly's hand, interlocking his fingers with hers, and smiled broadly.

"I have been wanting to do that the entire time. Do you mind?" he asked.

Carly's stomach was a flutter of butterflies at his touch, yet she loved the contact.

She looked into his eyes and said, "I don't mind."

Carly felt as though she was living in a picturesque movie. Daniel was everything she could have hoped for on a first date, their walk to the cupcake shop was in the bronze glow of sunset and she felt her heart leap with hope that she might possibly find love again after all her heartache.

At the cupcake shop, Carly ordered a simple vanilla cupcake that wouldn't stain her teeth while Daniel, completely oblivious to such precautions ordered a red velvet with red frosting on top.

They sat inside the shop as they ate their cupcakes and talked about everything. Carly shared how she was working so she could afford to pay for her college tuition, and how she was ready to move on from her hometown. She found herself thinking how strange it was to be able to share so much of her thoughts and dreams with a man she barely knew, but Daniel was different from any guy she had ever met. He was charming and gorgeous, but it was the open and guileless way he spoke about himself and his life that sparked her own openness.

Long before the cupcakes were gone, Carly knew that she wanted a second date with Daniel.

As they walked back to their cars at the steakhouse parking lot, Carly noticed that the area was much emptier and that if Daniel were anything like Kyle she could be in real danger. She hated herself for panicking. Daniel had been a perfect gentleman and was clearly nothing like the scumbag Kyle was, yet her heart was pounding, all of her senses were on hyper-alert, and she felt herself reach for her keychain which also held her small can of pepper spray.

"Well, this is me," Carly said as she pointed to her car.

As they walked to her car, Daniel blurted out, "Hey, I had a great time tonight. This has been an incredible day for me. Would you like to go out again sometime?"

After a short pause, she replied, "Me too. I would love that. Just call me and we can work out the details later." Carly turned quickly to unlock her car and open her door. She tossed in her purse and then felt that she may have been rude by how abruptly she was trying to leave, when she turned around, she was surprised to find Daniel on his cell phone saying, "You said to call you to work out the details for our next date. What are you doing tomorrow night?" He grinned broadly and then hung up.

"I can't wait till you call me back," he said sweetly before putting his phone back in his pocket. He reached out to give Carly a hug, but her body went stiff as he gently embraced her before pulling her door more open and watching her get into her car.

As Carly drove home that night, she couldn't help but think about how wonderful that date was. Daniel had been the perfect gentleman, and it seemed clear to Carly that he wasn't acting a part or pretending to be anything other than himself.

Carly was surprised to find herself crying as she drove home. *Why am I crying?* she thought aloud. She realized that the comparison between her date that night with how awful her entire junior year had been because of how bad her date with Kyle had been made her miss all that she had been robbed. She wished so desperately that she had never met Ryan or let him steal her innocence and then rob her of her dignity. How much of her life was taken away from her because of the perversion of one boy? If Ryan had never filmed her to raise money for his college tuition, Kyle wouldn't have the wrong idea of her and then spread malicious slander about her to her whole school. If he hadn't ruined her reputation, she might have been able to have more wonderful experiences like her date tonight. She had been a victim to the warped and evil acts of men and she let herself cry unabated at the misery of what had been stolen from her. Carly believed that time and future experiences could never undo or change the damage that had been done in her life. *I am permanently tainted,* she thought.

By the time Carly pulled into the driveway at her house, she found herself wanting to inflict the same pain on Kyle that he had done to her. She was seething with rage and believed that the only way to get control over her life was to make sure that jerks like Kyle had no power to harm other girls ever again. It had taken Carly one great date to make her realize that Kyle really should have been reported to the police. That she should have tried to report Ryan for the harm he had caused. She had suffered in silence because she was so mortified at what had happened to her and agonized by the perpetual abuse she experienced daily at school, she couldn't bring herself to face what had been done to her, but Carly was older now and she felt ready to get her justice.

As Carly walked into her house, she decided that she would be spending the night researching how to bring Kyle and Ryan to any sort of legal justice.

Chapter 5: Mixed Emotions

C arly had spent most of the night searching internet databases, and highlighting lawyer phone numbers in the yellow pages. She felt confused and exhausted when she was woken up to the sound of her mother pounding on her door at 8 a.m. asking if she wanted coffee while it was fresh.

"No, Mom. Go away! I'm sleeping!" Carly half-growled, half-whined. She had wanted the answers she sought to be simple and straightforward, but all she found was that she would need to invest a lot of time finding physical evidence of the harm Kyle had caused her in order to see him brought to justice. She also learned that Ryan had deleted his account on the seedy website and all video evidence of her was gone as far as she could tell. The misery he had inflicted was permanent in her life, and yet according to the law, there was now no evidence of a crime. She had waited too long and been too foolish, and she hated herself for that.

To Carly's mind, it felt like the law was bent on protecting abusers and making the victims suffer even more. Kyle could attempt rape or even rape more girls and unless someone went straight to the hospital and called the police to collect evidence, that girl would be scarred for life and absolutely nothing would happen to Kyle. He could just go on with his life, possibly abusing more victims.

Even worse was that Ryan had changed his number, and no longer seemed to exist on social media anywhere, despite the fact that she had created a spam account to search for him. It was like he just disappeared. Trying to hunt him down and get justice for what he had done to her felt like a dead end since she hadn't thought to take any screenshots or save the evidence of his crimes. After the crushing realization that Ryan would get away with what he did, Carly decided to focus all of her energy on Kyle.

Anger burning inside of her made it impossible to fall back asleep, and she laid on her bed with her mind reeling.

Suddenly, Carly had a thought. She would find Sara O. at school tomorrow and see if she could take her to coffee that afternoon. If Sara would agree to corroborate her story and they came forward about Kyle's abuse, maybe she could get justice for the damage he had caused to her life. Maybe she could even have the police check his computer for evidence of what Ryan had done.

She wondered if she should tell her principal about what Kyle had done to her. It was a year after the event, and Kyle had already graduated, but the harassment from the football players still happened, albeit far less regularly thanks to the rumors Sara and her friend Lindsay had started about them. Carly found herself being consumed with a burning desire to ruin Kyle's life as he had ruined hers.

With a groan, she got up and went to see if she could grab some freshly brewed coffee after all.

When she got to the coffee pot, she saw that her mom had not made any extra for her. "What the heck!?" You force me to wake up and then you don't have the decency to at least make extra coffee?!" Carly was furious and was clearly taking it out on her mom.

"Carly, you yelled at me to leave you alone. You made yourself very clear that you would be sleeping in. I was just following your demands. Don't blame me if you changed your mind. I am not a mind reader." Heidi sounded irritated and indignant.

"I'm sorry Mom, I just have a lot on my mind this morning," Carly apologized.

"Oh no! Did your date with the volunteer guy not go well?" Heidi probed.

"Oh no, it was amazing! Daniel was the perfect gentleman and we are probably going to go out again tonight." Heidi looked surprised at Carly's open assessment of her date.

Usually, Carly was secretive and surly when Heidi tried to talk about boys.

"It's just that I realized that one bad date almost a year ago caused me a lot of misery for this past year, and now that I want to press charges for the harm caused, it's probably too late." Angry tears slipped down Carly's face.

Carly didn't know what had come over her. Why was she telling her mom all of this? She usually never shared these sorts of details with her mom because Heidi wasn't the most sympathetic when it came to relationships with men. Her own wounding made her cynical and sharp.

"Do you mean Kyle?" Heidi said pointedly

"Yup that's the loser who got away with assault," Carly said irritably as she wiped her hot angry tears away. "Look, Mom, I just spent the whole night trying to figure out if I even have a case and it seems like because I took so long to come to my senses and try to stop him, no court will accept my evidence and he gets to get away with his crimes to go and assault some other poor girl." Carly's angry tears were flowing freely again. Her shoulders were low with the hopelessness she was feeling.

"OK... Well, let's try to put this out of mind for today since no lawyer's office is going to take your call on a Sunday anyway. We can worry about how to seek justice tomorrow." Heidi did something Carly never expected, she set down her cup of coffee, came over, and hugged Carly.

"It's just not fair." Carly cried into Heidi's shoulder. "Why am I being punished for someone else's crimes?"

Heidi stroked Carly's hair soothingly and said, "I know sweetheart, I know. Men are selfish and thoughtless of who they hurt," Heidi soothed.

Carly knew all too well what her mom's experience with a selfish and thoughtless man had been. Her mom had been left a single young mother because her dad had decided that he couldn't be faithful and had cheated on her while she was pregnant and then again after Carly was born. He had ultimately left her mom for a younger and dumber woman. In fact, her dad, Nick, was now on his fourth wife and Shellie was only thirteen years older than Carly.

"I think we should go to church today," Heidi said unexpectedly.

Carly rolled her eyes. "Mom, the nail chapel doesn't count as an actual church," she said as she used her shirt sleeves to wipe her eyes.

Heidi laughed as Carly knew exactly what she meant by her quirky comment. "They wash your feet; they uplift your spirit. What's so different about this chapel than any other church?" Heidi teased.

Carly and Heidi used to go to a local Baptist church when she was little, but when the elders of the church found out that Heidi was dating a man from the church, they told her she had to stop because it would lead to adultery. Utterly offended by their condemnation,

Heidi cussed them all out for being hypocritical pigs, and she and Carly had never stepped foot into another church since then, unless of course, you counted the Nail Chapel salon.

"I could use a pedicure before my date tonight," Carly said as she remembered that she had totally forgotten to call Daniel back the previous night because she had been in such a fog of hate, anger, and pain.

Carly set down her empty mug and ran to her room, leaving Heidi stunned by her sudden change of behavior.

"I have to call Daniel back," she yelled from her bedroom.

"Want me to make you coffee?" Heidi offered.

"Yes, please! You're the best!" Carly yelled back.

As the phone rang, Carly felt nervous. *What if Daniel was too offended by how long it took her to respond? What if it was too early and he wasn't awake? What if he was at church and she was embarrassing him with her call?* Her mind raced with all the what-ifs.

"Hello?" Daniel's deep voice seemed oddly off.

"Hi Daniel, it's Carly, is this a good time?" Carly said sweetly.

"Carly! I'm so glad you called. I actually just woke up, sorry if my voice is weird," Daniel said with a croaky voice.

Carly had been right. He had been asleep, and it was too early. She felt a slight twinge of guilt.

"I was beginning to worry you might not want to go out tonight," Daniel said as he cleared his throat.

"Oh, I'm sorry, I had a few things I had to take care of late last night and then I fell asleep. So, I decided to call you bright and early this morning," Carly said as cheerfully as she could muster.

"I was wondering if you wanted to go for a bike ride and maybe an ice cream afterwards," Daniel suggested.

"Or if that is too lame, then we can totally do anything else that you would enjoy." He added hastily.

Carly couldn't help but laugh at Daniel's obvious desire to provide her with a good time. She enjoyed being so admired.

"Daniel, I don't know if I am much of a biker. Plus, I don't think my bike is in working order. I haven't ridden it in at least two years and I'm pretty sure it's covered in spider webs in the back of my garage," Carly admitted.

Daniel didn't miss a beat, "Alrighty, I have crossed bike riding off the list. The next idea is to take you go-cart racing and potentially eat some greasy pizza from the nearby arcade," he said matter-of-factly.

Despite her anger and tears just minutes earlier, Carly found herself laughing again. His ideas were new and all sounded fun. "I think we have a winner," she said. "Just out of curiosity, what else did you have on your list?"

"Surfing, movie theater, bowling, mini golfing, you know just the usual," Daniel said playfully.

They both laughed.

"Well, I guess you have plenty more ideas to try out if things go well today." Carly teased.

"Actually, these are from my second date list. To hear the third date list, you'll have to play your cards right missy." Daniel teased back.

Carly worried that maybe Daniel was some type of player if he had lists for different dates. *Was it just a dumb joke or was he telling the truth?* she worried.

After a long pause, Daniel broke the silence. "So, can I pick you up at 4 p.m.?"

"Actually, I was hoping we could just meet there. My mom and I have this rule about dating. We don't share a car ride until after the third date when you have been totally vetted," Carly admitted.

"Your mom has some strict rules, but she clearly wants to keep you safe, and I totally understand. I'll text you the address and we can meet there at 4:30," Daniel replied.

"Sounds good. See you then." Carly hung up, and felt relieved that she hadn't blown her chances with Daniel.

The rest of the day went by in a blur. Carly and her mom enjoyed their pedicures and Carly was able to drive to the go-cart place with a few minutes to spare.

This time, instead of bringing a book, she brought the notebook she had been writing all of her research in. Carly knew that she was going to struggle to press any charges on Kyle that would actually get him arrested because she was stupid enough to not do it the day of the crime. She also knew that according to her school handbook bullying was only really dealt with when there was evidence or witnesses. She knew her friends would all back her up, but she was willing to bet that since the entire football team took part in her harassment, they would have more evidence saying that no bullying took place. She groaned at how impossible justice felt.

So far, her plans hinged on talking Sara O. into helping her get back at Kyle. They would start their own real rumors about the kind of scumbag he really was. And if she had any luck whatsoever, they would find hard evidence of Kyle's foul ways to take to the police and the school principal.

Carly looked at the dashboard clock in her car, it read 4:34 p.m.

"Shoot!" Carly exclaimed as she shoved her notebook under her driver's seat and grabbed her purse. In her plotting, she had lost track of time and was now running a little late. She and Daniel had agreed to meet at the ticket booth of the go-cart track at 4:30 p.m.

As she walked up to the booth, she saw Daniel talking to a pretty young woman who was dressed provocatively and flirting openly with him. Carly's heart sank. She was supposed to be on a date with this guy, and here he was chatting up some other girl. She stopped walking as she tried to figure out what to do.

The adult thing to do would be to ask Daniel to introduce her to this flirt. Maybe it wasn't what it looked like. Maybe she was his cousin? But then again, maybe things were exactly what they looked like, and maybe Daniel was just as girl-crazy and hormone-driven as all the other boys she knew. Maybe he was just another loser, and she was wasting her time getting her hopes up on him.

At that moment, Daniel looked up and saw her and began waving. His smile faded when they locked eyes. Carly's face must have given her away. He came toward her and Carly held her ground. She couldn't just run away now that she had been spotted.

"There you are!" Daniel said. "I got us the all-you-can-ride wristbands." He smiled. "You want me to put yours on you?"

Carly stood there. Her feet were glued to the concrete. She wanted to speak calmly, to not snap at him, and to not appear to be unjust or overly cynical. "Who's your friend there?" she said innocently. "Is she going to be joining our date?" Her words were too sweet, like a Venus fly trap about to snap on its prey.

"My wha..?" Daniel said as he looked back at the very beautiful woman he was just talking to. "Oh, you mean Roxy?" He snorted, "Oh, no. She is definitely not invited. Between you and me, I was hoping she wouldn't see me when I got here. She's my dad's personal assistant and I am not a big fan of hers." Daniel confided.

"She looks to be a big fan of yours," Carly intoned.

"Oh, she's a big fan of money. And she will be whatever she thinks she needs to be to get her claws into someone with money," Daniel whispered as he came close to Carly.

Carly looked into Daniel's eyes. She needed to know the truth. She needed to know if this guy was just like all the rest. Daniel seemed calm, open, and honest.

"So why is she here? Carly asked.

"No idea," Daniel said. "She asked me about my dad and family. I think she is trying to start an affair with my dad, but he's not into her."

"It looked more like she was hoping to start an affair with you," Carly blurted before she could stop herself.

At this, Daniel bellowed a hardy laugh. "Oh Carly. You are worth a thousand of Roxy," he said wholeheartedly. "You have integrity, grit, and intelligence. You are completely gorgeous and I promise, you have nothing to worry about when it comes to her."

Carly felt flattered. She wanted to believe Daniel. She wanted to trust him and to not let her past get in the way. *"He's different, remember?"* She told her heart. She decided that she was going to try and forget what she saw. She was here for a date and for fun. Daniel had already purchased the wristbands and she was just letting her past haunt her.

As she glanced back to the spot where Roxy had been, she found that she was now flirting with some other man who looked to be in his late forties and was accompanied by his teenage son. Maybe Daniel was right about her.

Smiling up at Daniel, Carly said, "Completely gorgeous huh?"

Daniel smiled, sunk his hands into Carly's hair to look her square in the face, and breathed, "The most beautiful woman I've ever met." He looked like he was going to kiss her. As much as Carly's stomach was fluttering, and she wouldn't have minded this handsome man kissing her, she had principles to protect her. She grabbed his hands, gently pulled them out of her hair, stepped back and said, "Wow, you sure know how to make a girl feel special."

Daniel was breathing a little faster. He smiled and pulled out the wristbands from his back pocket.

"You ready to get your butt kicked?"

Carly looked at the winding race track, then back at Daniel, and said, "You ready to eat my dust?"

Daniel laughed and then stepped closer to put her wristband on. Carly helped him put his on and the two stepped into the line.

After racing go-carts for about an hour, Carly and Daniel decided it was time to get dinner. When they walked into the pizza place attached to the arcade, the trilling sounds of arcade games hit Carly's ears and made the loud humming of the go-cart motors she thought had made her slightly deaf, seem like nothing. The noise in this place ensured that no one would even want to sit and linger. The blasting pop music intertwined with the yells and hoots of teenagers playing games, and the mechanical sounds and trilling chimes of points being won made Carly feel like she could hardly breathe. She looked over at Daniel to see how he felt.

Daniel mouthed something to her, but she couldn't hear him. She tried to tell him that she couldn't hear him, but she could hardly hear herself. Daniel grabbed her hand and walked out the door.

"Much better," he said a little too loudly. "I was asking if you would be open to eating somewhere else. That place is where you take a girl you don't want to see again, and well, I want to see you again." He smiled and wiggled his eyebrows.

"I would love to go somewhere else. I don't know how all those people could stand to be in that noise. It was overwhelming," Carly said as she breathed in deeply.

"There is an Italian place just up the road. We could probably just walk to it or if you want, we can drive," Daniel responded.

"Pasta sounds good. I don't know how far it is, so I'll let you decide if we walk or drive."

The way Daniel smiled at Carly's response and grabbed her hand told Carly he liked her answer.

"Let's walk. That way I have an excuse to hold your hand for longer." He grinned his broad handsome smile at her and Carly felt a strange and sudden desire to kiss him. She suppressed the foreign thought.

"Lead the way," Carly replied, returning the smile.

The Italian restaurant ended up being only five buildings down. It was way too fancy for what they were both wearing. Most of the men were in business attire and the wait staff seemed hesitant to want to serve two young people wearing sneakers and jeans. But Daniel knew how to make an impression and get good service. He went up to the hostess, gave her a $20, and said, "I would really appreciate it if you could find us a nice quiet table." She seemed a lot happier to serve him, now that she knew he was eager to pay.

"Yes sir, just one moment, and I'll have them prepare the best table."

Carly had not grown up with money. In fact, her mother and she rarely ate out, and when they did it was usually just ordering a pizza in. She had never known that people actually tip the hostess to get a table quickly. She suddenly felt like she needed to be on her best behavior. She didn't want Daniel to think she was some poor cleaning lady who didn't know anything about etiquette.

As they sat down in a cozy rounded booth, Daniel scooched in all the way so he could sit next to her. He leaned in and whispered in her ear, "I hope you don't mind, but these people are pretentious snobs and I think I am going to have to put them in their place for their judging looks based on our fashion choices."

Carly tilted her head ever so slightly and said, "What did you have in mind?"

"We need to order a lot of food. Please pick an appetizer that's the most expensive." He kissed her hand and then added "I'm paying for dinner and if you even attempt to offer, I swear I will kiss you right here in this booth." Carly saw the fire in his eyes and believed that he meant it.

She scooched a little further away from him and said "With such intimidating threats, I guess I have no choice." They both laughed at her attempt at a joke.

"If you'll excuse me, I need to use the restroom and freshen up a bit. I suggest you order the stuffed mushrooms and calamari for our starter." Carly got up to find the ladies' room.

When she walked into the bathroom on the other side of the restaurant, Carly was stunned to see Sara O. there in a cute little sundress applying a fresh coat of lipstick.

"Hi Sara," she said. She couldn't let this opportunity go. She had been wanting to talk to her, and here she was.

"Oh, hey... Carly." Sara looked her up and down and then said, "I'm guessing you didn't have a reservation here."

Carly laughed, "Oh, no. We just ended up here when our first dinner plans fell through."

"Figures. They are usually pretty strict about the dress code." How did you even get seated wearing that? I mean, I'm not trying to be rude, but my family has been coming here for years, and my parents always make me wear a dress."

"Oh, well, I guess the restaurant has loosened up a bit. They didn't seem to mind when my date and I walked in like this," Carly lied. She knew Daniel had tipped the hostess, but she couldn't stand the condescending way Sara was talking to her.

"So, you come here every Sunday with your family?" Carly asked.

"Unfortunately," Sara huffed. "Look, I've been hiding in here for at least five minutes, I should probably be getting back."

"Wait!" Carly practically shouted as Sara reached for the door. "Before you go, I wanted to ask you something." Carly took that moment to quickly tell Sara about her date experience with Kyle, and how she had wanted to press charges, but that it was too late now. She asked if Sara knew of any other girls that he may have harmed in the past year that she could talk to.

Sara was visibly stunned. Her mouth hung open and her eyes were wide. "I knew he was a total jerk when he said the stuff that he did, but I had no idea he had tried to... you know." She finally said before continuing on. "I only went out with him for a few months. I never had the problem that you had, but I know he said he dated a few girls after you. I think it was Naomi West and Kim Woodhall. Come to think of it, they are both Sophomores this year, so that might have been why he was able to date them so easily. Most of the girls that were in his grade and ours knew to avoid him because of the drama with you."

Carly gave her a questioning look as if to say, *"If you knew this, then why did you date him?"* and without having to say anything Sara replied, "I was trying to date a bad boy to piss off my dad. But like I said, it didn't last long. Kyle was weird."

Carly thanked Sara for listening and for the names. She quickly washed her hands and touched up her makeup. She was embarrassed to find that they had been in the bathroom for close to ten minutes.

When she came back to the table Daniel was talking genially to a very attractive waitress. Carly's red flag warning bells started to go off, but when she got closer, she could hear what he was saying.

Apparently, Daniel had taken her absence as an opportunity to order food for them both.

"Anything else sir?" the sumptuous waitress said sultrily.

"Nope, that ought to be more than enough for my date and me."

Carly smiled as she slid into the booth and sat down next to him.

"Did you order for me as well?" she asked.

Daniel waited for the waitress to walk away before telling her, "Well, the oh-so-helpful waitress seemed insistent on waiting for me to decide, so it seemed like the easiest way to get rid of her."

"I'm sorry that I took so long. I ran into an old friend in the restroom, and we lost track of time catching up," Carly said. It was important to her that Daniel didn't think she was in the restroom that long for other reasons.

Just then the stuffed mushrooms came as well as a couple of sodas. "I hope you don't mind, but I ordered you a Coke."

Carly smiled at his thoughtfulness. Daniel had a remarkable way of making her feel like she was a prized jewel in his eyes.

As each wave of food came, Carly found herself in more shock. It seemed like Daniel had ordered her at least four entrees.

"Daniel, how much food do you think I can eat?" she said in surprise as their table was filled with dinner plates.

"Oh that." He laughed. "Well, you only ordered a salad last time so I wasn't entirely sure what you would like best. I ordered all 8 of the main courses so you could take whichever you like. I figure, we will sample them all and then we can eat the leftovers all week."

This was a fancy restaurant and Daniel had easily just spent a few hundred dollars just on the main dishes. Carly was impressed, but that small nagging voice told her to be careful, to keep her guard up, and that all of this was so he could justify trying to use her.

She tried not to let those nagging thoughts interfere with the incredible feast he had ordered for them. But with her plans for getting justice and her fears from past experiences, she wasn't her usual flirty self.

"Hey is everything OK?" Daniel asked as he took a sip of his soda.

"Yes, everything is delicious. Why? Don't you think so?" Carly responded trying to play ignorant to the real meaning of his question.

"No, I mean... Well, it's just that you have been a little quiet tonight and I was worried that you were thinking about the whole Roxy fiasco," he stammered out.

"Oh, that. No, I believed you. I was just thinking about some girls from my school that my friend Sara and I had talked about when I was in the restroom. Turns out they had both dated a real creep of a guy, and I guess it really scarred them."

Daniel gazed thoughtfully at her. "That's terrible. Do you want to talk about it?"

His entire face and countenance spoke of the genuine open nature of his question. It wasn't a trap or some form of manipulation. He really cared about what was bothering her and making her less chatty.

"It's a little too heavy for a second date. But the gist is we think that this creep sexually assaulted our two friends. He got away with it because they were too ashamed to talk about it or report him," Carly whispered. She could hardly believe she was telling Daniel this, but he had that effect on her. He made her want to be open and honest with him.

Daniel dropped his fork mid-bite. "What? And this guy hasn't faced any charges or repercussions? They need to report him to the police!"

"It might be too late. This happened several months ago, so they won't have any physical evidence against him anymore," Carly said somberly.

"Even if they don't have enough to prosecute, it's important that there is a record on file so that if another girl gets harmed and is courageous enough to go directly to the police, they will take her much more seriously because there are statements of previous crimes on his record." Daniel sounded passionate and stern.

"I didn't know it worked like that," Carly said thoughtfully.

"Well, I am not 100% sure myself, but doing nothing is definitely worse! How many more girls will this loser assault until someone finally comes forward?"

Daniel's passion for justice against Kyle made Carly's heart pound. She was wrong to be afraid that he was trying to buy her favors. She was wrong to think he could ever be anything close to the nightmare that Kyle was. Before she knew what she was doing she found herself pulling his shirt toward her and kissing him.

It was a sweet, gentle kiss that she found herself wishing could just go on and on, but she forced herself to pull away quickly.

"Sorry. It's just that you're one of the good ones, and I guess I couldn't resist," she said sheepishly.

Daniel, with eyes still half closed looked like he wished it hadn't ended either. "Don't apologize. That was a wonderful surprise! Feel free to do it again," he said as he looked into her eyes. He ran his fingers through her hair and then cleared his throat, straightened up and said, "I think it's time for the bill and to box all of this up."

Carly smiled and said, "What, too stuffed for dessert?"

"I think I already had mine, thanks." He leaned in and kissed her again. It was intoxicating and if not for her dislike of public displays of affection, Carly would have made out with him right then and there.

The sultry and flirty waitress came over to see how everything was and was no longer speaking only to Daniel. She seemed to be trying a new tactic of earning a good tip by complimenting Carly while she boxed up their leftovers.

As they left the restaurant with four bags of leftovers, Carly and Daniel both seemed to want to get to their cars quickly. They talked about their plans for the week, what work and school would look like and Daniel made plans to work late on Wednesday and Friday, so he could sneak some kisses from Carly while she was supposed to be working.

When they got to Carly's car, Daniel put the bags of leftovers in her backseat and said, "I would very much like to stay and kiss you, but I know it's getting late and honestly, I'm not sure if I could get myself to stop once we got started." He leaned in closer to her and breathed her scent in. Carly found herself fighting the urge to start kissing him all over again. Daniel's respect and the gentlemanly way he treated her made her want him in a way she didn't think she could ever feel again.

"Thank you for a wonderful night," Carly whispered. "I look forward to seeing you on Wednesday." He kissed her hand and then shut her driver's side door before walking to his truck.

Carly drove home that night feeling like life was bliss. She had a plan for making sure that Kyle got what he deserved, and she was dating the hottest, kindest man in the world. This was the best life had felt in years.

Chapter 6: The Plan for Justice

On Monday morning, Carly groaned as she looked at the time on her alarm clock. She got up quickly and immediately began rushing to get ready for school. The previous night, after she had gotten home from her date with Daniel, she had immediately called Darcy to tell her all about it. Darcy had been in the middle of studying for her math test, but still had made time to talk about Carly's date, and the two of them had even hatched the plan to carpool to school every morning. Darcy's mom had come into her room when they were talking, and after Darcy gave her the quick rundown of their ideas, she had approved of their carpool plans, adding that she would also pay Carly $20 a week for gas money. Carly felt as though maybe, just maybe, her luck was changing. Senior year felt like it was going to be her comeback year.

As Carly rushed to get ready for her day, she couldn't help but find her mind drifting back to that kiss with Daniel and how much her life seemed different all because of him. She couldn't have predicted a few short weeks ago that she would be happily dating the best guy ever and earning an easy $20 a week by sharing a ride with her best friend to school. Even her plans for getting justice against Kyle seemed to be lucky. Because she had gone on a great date with Daniel, she was able to run into Sara and get the information she needed. Because of Daniel, she was emboldened to make a police report about her incident with Kyle and to try to convince the other two girls to do the same, if they had also been assaulted. It felt as if everything good in her life at that moment directly resulted from saying "yes" to Daniel. Carly laughed as she thought to herself, *He's my good luck charm.* She wondered what Jessica would have to say when she learned just how wrong she had been about Daniel.

Just as Carly was finishing the final touches of her makeup for the day, her phone began to ring. She raced from her bathroom mirror to her room to answer, thinking it might be Daniel.

"Hello?" she said a little breathily.

"Hey girl, I'll be over in two minutes. Consider this call your warning to be ready," Darcy said playfully.

"I am just now packing my backpack and getting my shoes on. I'll meet you at my car," Carly said hurriedly and then hung up. It wasn't unusual for Darcy and Carly to hang up without saying goodbye. They often treated phone calls like sending a voice memo.

Carly grabbed a slice of toast from her mother's plate and took a few gulps from her coffee before kissing her cheek and saying, "Bye!" as she ran out the door, leaving a bewildered-looking Heidi.

Just as Carly was slinging her backpack into the back seat, Darcy walked up. "Perfect timing, huh?" Carly said.

"Yup, but if we don't hurry, we risk being tardy for homeroom," Darcy said worriedly.

"I'll put the pedal to the metal," Carly enthused as the girls got in and buckled.

When they got to school, Darcy said, "I gotta run. It normally takes me five minutes to walk to my homeroom from here, and I am trying to have perfect attendance this year." Before Carly could say anything, Darcy had taken off running.

Usually, Carly would have turned on her iPod and blasted some of her favorite tunes, but this morning felt different. The birds were chirping, the sky was blue, and she felt like enjoying the day rather than trying to tune it out.

As she walked down the path between the tennis courts and the football field, she noticed that one of Kyle's old football buddies and some girl were only several feet ahead of her. Her heart started to race. She wasn't wearing her usual hoodie, which made it hard to identify her, or blasting her music, which made her unable to hear the taunts. She suddenly felt as though she were naked, and her breathing began to quicken.

Carly stopped walking to try and gather her thoughts and control her breathing. Her mind raced in different directions. On the one hand, she wanted to run back to her car and play hooky. She would never make the mistake of skipping her hoodie and headphones ritual ever again. On the other hand, she needed to know who that girl was and if this guy, who she vaguely remembered as Evan, was treating her right.

Carly took in a few controlled, slow breaths and then began walking toward her homeroom. She didn't have to face this Evan guy at the moment, but she resolved that if anyone taunted her, she was done lying down and just taking it. She was going to fight back. Just as she had decided this, the football jock and the unknown girl split up and went their separate ways to class. Her bravery hadn't been needed, but the decision Carly had made inside herself felt permanent.

Carly walked into homeroom just as the final bell for class rang out. It wasn't unusual for her to be barely on time, so no one even looked up at her. She made her way to her seat next to Jill and took out some of her homework that she was supposed to be finishing up.

"Morning!" rang Jill's bright, cheerful voice.

"Morning yourself," Carly replied happily.

"You seem bright this morning. Did you have a good weekend?" Jill said suspiciously.

"The best!" Carly exclaimed a little too loudly. She glanced around and noticed Mr. Rodriguez was too busy working on something and hadn't heard.

Homeroom was supposed to be a time when students got the daily news from the school and worked on their homework or whatever the school admin felt they should be doing, like test prep. Carly leaned a little closer to Jill and began to tell her everything, starting with meeting Daniel at work and then again at the beach clean-up. The two girls spent the entire thirty minutes of homeroom fully absorbed in Carly's romantic, whirlwind story.

As they walked out of class, Jill said, "Wow, Carly. I'm so happy that you found a good guy. Daniel sounds amazing, and I hope I get to meet him sometime."

One of the things that Carly had always loved about Jill was that she wasn't petty or jealous. When you had bad news, she really seemed to be upset for you. And when you had good news, she was just as happy and excited. Jill wasn't like so many of the other girls in the school who were fake, venomous snakes just pretending to be your friend until they could find some way to tear you apart. Jill wasn't stunningly beautiful; in fact, most people thought she was plain and unremarkable looking, but Carly thought Jill was gorgeous. When they first became close friends in their sophomore year, Carly had felt like Jill's kind heart and sweet ways made her stunning. Seeing her now, Carly wasn't sure why she ever felt like Jill had betrayed her when she asked questions about the incident with Kyle. She knew now that Jill would have only wanted to get to the bottom of things and do her best to help her. She wasn't asking questions because she didn't believe Carly! Carly groaned internally at the realization of her blunder. Several months of lost time with her closest friends was just another thing Kyle had stolen from her. Another debt he owed her. She felt the anger boiling inside her. She hated Kyle for the demon-spawn that he was. Carly hated all of his pathetic loser friends who chose to follow in his gross, perverted footsteps rather than try to put an end to her humiliation and terror. She vowed to herself that she would never let a guy hurt her like that ever again. She would never take a beating like that silently. She was going to fight back, and she would win or die trying.

By lunchtime, Carly found that she had a headache. She had been gritting her teeth in anger for hours. Her burning desire to find Naomi and Kim and to get justice for what she went through was all-consuming, and she hadn't been able to focus on her classes. When she got to the benches, she knew she didn't have the patience to wait for her friends to come to their lunch spot with their cafeteria trays. Carly's heart burned with her mission for justice, so she pulled out her phone and texted Jill and Darcy, *"I have to do something during lunch. Be back soon."*

She knew Kim ate near the tennis courts with her friends, so she headed in that direction.

She had rehearsed in her head what she would say a million times. "Hi Kim, I'm Carly. I wanted to know if I could talk to you for a minute about Kyle." Carly was infamous at school and felt like she didn't need to say anything more than that. If Kim was open to helping her, that should be enough.

Kim was where she was told she would be. Carly had researched by flipping through last year's yearbook and finding out who Kim hung out with. Emboldened by her need for justice, she had also spent time that day asking anyone she thought might be Kim's friend where she hung out.

Carly walked up and noticed that Kim was sitting down eating. She wasn't talking to anyone around her and even had her headphones on. Carly felt like she was looking through a weird type of mirror.

She squatted down in front of Kim and waved to get her attention. Kim saw her but glared and went back to staring down and playing with her lunch.

Carly was not going to be put off so easily. She took the headphones off of Kim's head and whispered, "I know what you're doing, and it isn't going to ever get better like this. If you really want to feel better, come with me and listen to what I have to say."

"What are you talking about!?" Kim said irritably.

"I'm Carly Morales, and I want to talk to you about putting a stop to Kyle. Forever."

With that, Carly handed back the headphones, stood up, and walked ten feet away to the path next to the tennis courts. She turned back to see if Kim would come, and much to her satisfaction, Kim was also getting up to follow her.

When the two girls reached the end of the path near the parking lot, Carly turned around to make sure no one was close enough to overhear them.

"I want to tell you the story of what Kyle did to me because I suspect, based on your hoodie and headphones, that you share a similar trauma story."

As she told Kim the details of that horrible night and the tormenting gossip and taunts of the following year, Kim's eyes went wide.

"Why didn't you ever tell anyone? Why didn't you report him?" Kim asked.

"Because I was ashamed and weak. But I'm not weak anymore, and I want us to make sure Kyle can never harm another girl ever again," Carly said passionately.

"He didn't violate me, Carly. He took me out and put the moves on me just like you, but I panicked and froze. I tried telling him no, but we were in his car. He didn't stop so I just sort of let him until he finished with me." At this confession, Kim burst out in tears.

Carly grabbed Kim and gave her a tight hug. "Just because you didn't fight back doesn't mean he had your permission. Did you want that to happen?" Carly asked, looking into Kim's tear-stained face.

Kim shook her head vehemently.

"That's what I thought." Carly let go of Kim and began telling her the plan.

"First, we have to find Naomi West: she's another victim. Then, we all have to write down our statements and take them to the police. After that, we all have to give the principal a copy of our statements. Even if it is too late for our statements to get Kyle arrested, or hurt him in any official way, we can move on to making him a social pariah. No girl will ever fall for his crap ever again. Even his ex-girlfriend Sara is on our side."

Kim stopped walking. "I don't want to talk to Naomi." Her tone was firm and angry.

"Why not?" Carly said gently.

"Naomi used to be my friend. We were both on the tennis team. Then, one day, she started dating Kyle. We would all hang out sometimes. He seemed funny and nice, but after we went to a party where some drinking was happening, she just stopped talking to me. In fact, she flat-out ignored me. A month later, Kyle did what he did to me."

Carly took a moment to take in what Kim had just told her and what she suspected had happened at that party.

"Kim, I think Kyle probably harmed Naomi at that party. It fits his personality and her change in behavior after it. I know this is painful, and believe me, I want nothing more than to wake up from this nightmare, but we can't. You know your life isn't OK after what he did. You know that he needs to face the consequences of his crimes. We can't just let him keep getting away with it. Think about the next girl, the one who isn't miserable like us. I should have done this a year ago. If I had been braver, maybe I could have stopped Kyle from hurting you and Naomi. But I was hurting and I shut down when I should have fought."

Carly was now sobbing. Kim stared at her a long moment before saying, "Carly, I know what they said about you and what you had to face at school every day. I used to laugh at their crude jokes and join in. I never thought about how you might have felt or if what they said was even true or not. I'm sorry you had to go through all of that. I can't imagine how terrible I would feel if everyone was making fun of me after what happened." She gave Carly a quick hug, then rubbed her arms as if to try and make her stop crying.

"I know where to find Naomi. She hides in the girls' locker room all of lunch period so she doesn't have to see or hear anyone," Kim said.

When Carly and Kim got to the locker room, the first bell to signal the end of lunch rang. "We have to be quick!" Carly said as she ran inside.

She looked all around the locker room and bathrooms but without success. Naomi was nowhere in sight.

"Tomorrow, at the start of lunch, let's meet back here and try again," Carly told Kim.

Kim nodded in agreement, and the two girls went their separate ways to get to class.

All the rest of that day, Carly felt like she had won a victory. Yet she still had trouble concentrating on anything other than her plan for justice.

As Carly and Darcy drove home, Carly shared how she had spent her lunch and planned on finally getting justice for what Kyle did to her. To her surprise, Darcy was not as supportive as she thought she should be.

"I think it's a really good idea to make a statement to the police and to tell the principal, but the part where you plaster the internet, and school hallways with his yearbook photo and the stuff about what a creepy perv he is seems like it might be going too far," Darcy said carefully.

Carly couldn't believe her ears. "Are you serious right now?! Going too far? He's the guy who stole a year of my life. He stole the joy from Kim and me, and he is going around ruining innocent girls' lives! He has to be stopped. This is just the tip of the iceberg of what I am prepared to do to ensure no girl ever lets herself be alone with him ever again!" Carly raged.

The radio hummed music in the long pause before Darcy responded.

"I know he ruined a year of your life. I know he deserves to be put in jail. I am on your side here. I just feel like you spending a lot of your time posting what happened won't get you that year back or undo what he did. I feel like it's just going to make you have to relive the pain over and over." Darcy seemed genuinely concerned, and her worried expression softened Carly a little.

"Darc, I have to relive the pain of that year no matter what. I tried to ignore it and walk away from it, but all it did was rob me of my life for the past year. Maybe, if I fight back, I can ensure that he never hurts anyone again, and maybe when I have my justice, I will finally feel like the sun shines on my skin again. I am tired of hiding in the shadows, tired of feeling so much pain that I shut out everything, and then I'm just numb. I want to live my life again. Can't you understand that?"

"I just don't want to see you suffer more than you already have. You're my best friend, and I support you. I just want to know that you're thinking about all of the ways he will try to fight back," Darcy said gently.

"Thanks for being on my side, even if you don't fully understand it." Carly smiled weakly.

That evening, Carly wrote out her statement of events. The lawyer that her mom had her call for a free consultation said she needed to keep it as factual as possible and avoid any language or descriptions that weren't rooted in objective facts.

Stating only the facts turned out to be much harder than Carly had thought. Her blood boiled with each sentence she wrote, and she scrawled foul names describing the kind of person she felt Kyle was. Carly spent most of her time that afternoon reworking her letter, and it wasn't until she felt it was ready to show to Kim and Naomi, as well as the police, that she realized she had a mountain of homework she still needed to do, but couldn't because she had to leave for work and wouldn't be able to work on any of it until after her shift. She had a test the next morning that she needed to study for and found herself crying over the fact that she would be up until at least 1 a.m. She raged at the injustice of how Kyle's choice to assault her meant she was constantly suffering. *Why was life always so unfair?! Why did bad people get away with their crimes while good people just suffered the consequences of it?* Her heart was filled with the sour bitterness of hate and a deep-rooted desire to see Kyle punished. If she was honest with herself, she didn't really want justice; she wanted revenge. Carly wanted Kyle's life to be miserable for as long as he lived. She wanted him to know what it was like to live in the darkness of shame and misery. She wanted to make sure he never enjoyed another day of his life ever again.

Chapter 7: Following Through

The next morning, Carly was so shaky and groggy when she woke up that she almost missed the sunlight shining through her blinds, indicating that she had clearly overslept. As she got up and rubbed her eyes, she noticed a pounding coming from her front door and realized that it must have been what woke her up. As Darcy pounded on her front door, she yelled, "Come on, Carly! Wake up!" Normally, Heidi would have answered the door, but she had left early this morning to prepare to interview several candidates for her business.

"Just a second!" Carly yelled back to the front door, where Darcy was still hammering away. Carly began her mad dash of shoving books in her school bag, taking just a moment's pause to ensure that her statement of facts about Kyle was also there. She rushed to grab her shoes and walked out the door, still wearing her work attire she had fallen asleep in.

"Whoa! Everything OK?" Darcy exclaimed in surprise when she saw the state of Carly.

"Yeah, let's just get to school. I have a test right after homeroom and I don't want to make you late," Carly mumbled through a yawn.

Carly, you can't drive like this." She gestured to Carly's half-sleeping stance. "You need to chug some coffee and at least change your shirt or something." Darcy walked past Carly into the house and made a beeline for the kitchen.

Carly's exhaustion made her slow to respond to Darcy, who was now grabbing a canister of Folgers coffee and preparing a fresh pot. "Are you sure? I don't want to ruin your perfect attendance," Carly said groggily.

"I'll be fine arriving late, but I might die if I let you try to drive like this," Darcy said playfully, gesturing to all of Carly. "Besides, you look like a train wreck -no offense! Maybe you could take these next few minutes to brush your teeth and change your outfit?" Darcy said it like a question, but Carly knew she was just trying to be nice.

Carly shut the front door and dropped her backpack where she stood before she went to freshen up.

In less than ten minutes, the two girls walked back out with travel mugs full of hot, steamy energy. Carly's freshly brushed hair, new outfit, and a dab of makeup had worked wonders on her appearance. She looked awake and prepared for the day. Darcy wondered aloud, "How do you manage to go from stinky zombie to gorgeous girl so fast?"

Carly just laughed. It seemed ridiculous that her fresh jeans and t-shirt, a spritz of perfume, and a three-minute effort of makeup could do anything as drastic as Darcy made it seem. "I think this magical bean potion you made for us must have transformed me," she joked back.

When they got to school, the student parking lot was devoid of any students, and when Darcy checked her watch, she realized they were exactly eleven minutes late. "We are going to have to visit the front office to get passes to class. Otherwise, Ms. Simmons is going to send me straight back out, and I'll get detention," Darcy whined slightly.

"Sorry, Darcy. I guess I messed up. I was up all night working on my statement and then trying to prepare for a test today." Carly yawned and took a large gulp of coffee.

"Nothing we can do about it now except face it." Darcy grinned her kind smile back at Carly. "At least we are in it together."

The two girls walked to the front office to accept their tardy marks and get their passes to class. Passes were how their school dealt with late students, who their teachers had marked as absent. If you didn't check in at the front office, you were counted as absent for your homeroom, and that meant your parents would get a phone call by your first class to say you skipped out on school.

By the time Carly made it to homeroom, the bell to dismiss them was just about to ring. Mr. Rodriguez took her note and told her to take a seat. Jill looked up and smiled before noticing that something seemed off about Carly.

"Are you OK?" Jill asked in concern.

"Yeah, just had a long night and slept in too late," Carly replied as she let out another yawn.

Just then, the bell signaling the end of homeroom rang out. The two girls got up and walked out with the rest of the class.

"Will I see you at lunch today?" Jill asked hopefully.

"Probably not today. I have some stuff I have to take care of. But I should have it wrapped up by tomorrow," Carly yelled back as she walked away from Jill quickly to get to her next class.

When Carly arrived at her first-period class to take her test, she noticed that she had completely forgotten to put her page of notes in her binder. She groaned as she realized her mistake. She had spent so much of the night preparing those notes to help her with this test, and now, because of the trauma she was trying to move past, she would have to take this test without her notes. She felt utterly depressed. This year was supposed to be her year. But so far, senior year felt like a weird part two of her junior year. She wanted to make sure she got a 4.0 GPA this year because she needed to get into college so that she could escape her hometown. If Kyle stole that from her as well, she vowed she would devote the rest of her life to ruining his.

As Mrs. Fitzpatrick handed out her history test, Carly hoped she would retain enough of what she studied the night before to at least pass the test. She didn't know why she did it, but she found herself mumbling a prayer, "God, help me." Jill was always saying little prayers like that around her, so maybe that was where she got it from, but after she said it, she found she felt a little calmer. She liked the idea of a loving God and had even gone to church with Jill a couple times over the years, but when she went back home to her life and her problems, it was hard to feel like a good and loving God existed.

The test went smoother than she would have thought. To her amazement, it was all multiple-choice, and she had always been a good multiple-choice test taker. Carly wondered if it was her little prayer or if all that studying she had done right before falling asleep had paid off.

When lunch finally came around, Carly went straight to the girls' locker room to meet Kim, with the hope that they would find and convince Naomi to report Kyle with them. It was a solid ten minutes of waiting by the door before Kim showed up.

"What took you so long?" Carly demanded.

"Sorry, I needed to buy my lunch first. I was up most of the night working on my statement like you told me to, and I didn't get a chance to pack my lunch," Kim said while chewing on a large bite of a soft pretzel.

"I understand that," Carly said as her stomach gave a low rumble. "I have been so focused on getting through this that I forgot to eat or even think about food."

Kim handed her the Granny Smith apple from her lunch tray. "I don't like this kind of apple. Would you like it?"

Carly didn't particularly care for the sweet and usually mushy lunch apples, but she took the apple gratefully as she realized just how hungry she was.

"Let's go in and look for Naomi again," Carly said before taking a large bite out of the apple. It was mushy, just as she had expected.

"Oh, I forgot to tell you. I messaged several people last night and asked about her. Apparently, she told her parents all that happened with Kyle." Kim said as she chewed a bite of her lunch. "No one was too sure about what actually happened between them, but a few of her friends confirmed that her parents pulled her out of school before the end of last year because of it. She transferred to a private school," Kim said as she stuffed another bite of her lunch into her mouth. "I guess our falling out before that made me not notice," she said through a mouthful of food.

Carly felt a surge of emotions. She was jealous that Naomi had parents who would listen to her and who loved and supported her; she was angry that she didn't. She was angry that her plan was weakening, but hopeful that Naomi's parents reported Kyle already. Carly tried to ignore the nagging feeling that perhaps all her efforts to get justice would fail.

"Thanks for doing some research," Carly said in what she hoped sounded genuine and calm.

"Do you still want to carry out the plan?" Kim asked skeptically.

"Yeah. Let's go make copies of our statements. We need to give each other a copy, and we can give the principal a copy, and then tomorrow after school, I can drive us to the police station, and we will submit our original statements to the police," Carly replied in a shaky voice.

She knew that she wanted this. She needed this, but she was terrified that no one would take them seriously.

The girls walked to the library, where a copier machine was, put their dimes in, and printed out three copies of each of their statements. Carly read over Kim's to make sure she had followed the instructions: no emotions, just straight facts about when, where, what, and how. The lawyer Carly's mom had called had given them some practical information on how to correctly report the incident so that it would be most impactful in court, should it ever come to that.

Satisfied that Kim had taken her advice seriously and that her statement was detailed, precise, and devoid of subjective terms, Carly gave Kim a nod of approval.

Minutes later they were sitting in the principal's office, and Carly could feel her heart pounding wildly. She was glad Kim was there with her; otherwise, she felt certain she would have chickened out and left.

Principal Heathers was a kindly-faced man with gray hair and a round nose who looked to be about sixty. He had been their school's principal for the last fourteen years, and before that, he had been a teacher for eighteen years. Principal Heathers asked them if they would like a peppermint from his candy dish. The two girls shook their heads, and he set the dish back down on his desk.

"Why don't you start at the beginning and tell me what happened," he said gently.

Carly and Kim looked at each other, and Carly nodded. Kim was visibly frightened and seemed only able to give a mild squeak.

"It's like this, sir," Carly began. "Last year, I was sexually assaulted by another student here. He and his friends bullied me so badly that I was too afraid to say anything or seek justice at the time. But I recently learned that he has continued to harm other girls; Kim Woodhall, next to me, and another student, who recently transferred to a different school to get away from him, Naomi West. When I learned that he was a serial offender, I knew I had to come forward so that Kyle could not harm more girls in the future."

With that, Carly took out a copy of her statement and signaled Kim to do the same. Principal Heathers seemed dismayed at what she said but took the statements from them. He put on his reading glasses and began to read them. His face gave little away, but Carly noticed that he turned a shade of red and seemed to be trying not to wince.

When Principal Heathers looked up after finishing reading their statements, he asked, "Have you taken these to the police?"

We are doing that later today," Carly lied. She was worried that perhaps he might try to protect Kyle so word didn't get out that an offender had graduated from their school.

"Good," Heathers said firmly. "I will need a full police report in order to take action. Kyle doesn't attend here any longer, so there is nothing I can do to him, but his friends that you mentioned, Carly, might still be able to receive consequences for their poor choices. I want to tell you both that I am sorry for the suffering you have experienced. I am proud of your bravery today, and I hope very much that you never go through anything as terrible as this again. I'll need a list of names from you Carly for the friends that also bullied you."

Carly had expected he might, and so she produced the list of the names of all the football players who had been instigators and key players of her harassment that she had prepared the night before.

Carly could hear her pulse in her ears as she sat with a stunned expression. She had believed for so long that Principal Heathers wouldn't care or do anything, that no one would take her side or believe her. She was relieved that things seemed to finally be going her way.

Kim spoke up and surprised them both, "Sir, did Naomi's parents explain what Kyle did to her? Did she get a police report? I just don't understand why Kyle never got expelled or punished."

"Miss Woodhall, I cannot give you information about another student. But I can say that had I been given a police report by them, I would have taken the same action I have stated to you. As it is, I will be arranging a parent meeting within the week with the members of the football team who participated in your ongoing harassment. We will discuss the charges laid against them, and there will be disciplinary steps taken."

His response made Carly feel uneasy. Of course, she wanted this, but to have so many people made aware of the cruel torture she suffered did little to ease her anxiety.

"If there is nothing further that you wish to discuss, I am afraid I have other matters to attend to. Please see Mrs. Howell on your way out, and she can give you both passes to class as our meeting has gone past the lunch hour."

The two girls got up and walked out of the principal's office in silence. Carly felt stunned at how easy that felt. Last year, when this had all happened, she was told she would have to have her parents meet with Kyle and his parents, and now that she had a written statement and was going to the police, it was all easy-peasy.

"Did that feel too easy to you?" Carly asked Kim.

"Easy?" Kim asked. "No, that felt mortifying. Having an old man like Principal Heathers read about Kyle violating me was humiliating and terrifying. There was nothing easy about that."

Carly gave Kim a quick hug to try to reassure her. "We did the right thing. I think we should try to go to the police station today after school. Can you call your mom and ask?"

Kim pulled out her cell phone and called her mom right then and there. Carly noticed that Kim didn't tell her mother what they were actually planning on doing. She just said that she needed to get some schoolwork done with her classmate Carly after school and that Carly would give her a ride home.

"All set," Kim said as she put her phone away. "She said as long as I am home by 5 p.m., that should be fine."

"Let's plan on meeting by the student parking lot right after school. I might have to drop a friend off at home before we go, but that won't take more than ten minutes or so," Carly said, and the two girls went their separate ways to class.

When school was out for the day, Carly quickly headed to her car to try to explain things to Darcy before she introduced her to Kim. Darcy's surprise was apparent, but Carly could see she was trying to be supportive.

When Kim showed up, Carly introduced her to Darcy and said, "Darcy and I carpool to school since we are neighbors. I just need to drop her off, and then you and I can go straight to the police station."

"Sounds like a plan," Kim responded as the three girls got into Carly's car.

Chapter 8: The Aftermath

Carly woke up the next morning to her alarm blaring and her head aching. She had cried herself to sleep, and her eyes felt gritty and puffy. It wasn't a sad cry, but rather a bitter, raging, angry cry. She and Kim had waited for over an hour to see a police officer to give their statements and report the crimes. The police officer, who took their statements and questioned them about what happened, was kind and appeared sympathetic. But when it came down to it, she told them that since these crimes happened too long ago to gather any physical evidence, it was unlikely that Kyle would face any jail time. She also mentioned that because Kyle had a clean record and came from a well-off family, it was also unlikely that he would have anything other than a lawyer bill that his parents would have to pay in the event that things did proceed to court.

Carly scrubbed at her aching eyes and tried to keep the anger and bitterness from coming back in wild sobs. She had waited too long to gather enough courage to fight back, and now, it didn't matter to anyone else that she was the victim. She looked at the police report in her hand and felt a little comforted. At least Principal Heathers would take action against the students who had been a part of Kyle's gang. Now, she would see a small measure of justice against the guys who had all made a sport of tainting her reputation and had made her junior year a living hell. Carly tried to calm her anxiety and assure herself that she would get justice from Kyle, one way or another. She and Kim had worked out a plan of listing the names of the guys that had participated in harassing her and enabling Kyle, and a brief statement of the kind of losers they all were. They had even agreed to post flyers all over the school that afternoon and would later post on social media under fake profiles. They had agreed to act quickly blasting the truth about Kyle and his group of followers so that they were first to speak out and the guys who would be facing repercussions with Principal Heathers wouldn't have time to make up more lies.

With effort Carly decided to get up and face the day. She got ready quickly and put on her black hoodie and loose jeans. It had always felt like her armor, and today she needed all the strength and courage she could muster. She felt as though she was going to fight a losing battle, but she knew that if she didn't fight for her justice, no one else would. They would all just watch her get bullied and traumatized day in and day out, and no one would ever do anything to protect her.

Fueled by her purpose, Carly organized her evidence meticulously. She placed her police report copy, the statement copies, and her mock-up of the flyer she and Kim would be distributing to as many lockers as possible in a black school folder. She was ready to take action, to make her voice heard. She did her best to eat breakfast. Carly hadn't felt like eating anything; her rage was still burning inside her belly, but she knew if she didn't, she would feel weak and unable to think clearly by the time lunch rolled around, so she forced herself to eat a fried egg on avocado toast.

"Knock, knock," Darcy's voice rang out.

"It's open," Carly tried to yell back through a steamy bite of break-fast.

"Oh! I take it things didn't go so well last night?" Darcy said, taking in Carly's black hoodie and furrowed eyebrows. She also noticed Carly's swollen eyes, and that she hadn't made any effort to her appearance. It almost felt like they had gone back in time to right after the date with Kyle.

"It went fine. Well, no, that's not true. It was humiliating to have to answer a ton of questions about what Kyle did to us and why we were only just now coming forward with our statements only to be told it was probably too late for us to get any real justice." Carly shoved her breakfast away from her with a look of disgust. She had a bad taste in her mouth that had nothing to do with her meal.

"Let's just get to school," Carly mumbled irritably as she slung her bag over her shoulder and headed for the door.

Darcy looked stunned by how upset Carly was. "I was worried this would be like picking a scab off an old wound. I just didn't think it would bring up this much pain and anger."

Darcy whispered, "Is there anything I can do?"

"I don't know!" Carly snapped. Tears started to fall down her face again as she got into her car and slammed her door shut.

The drive to school was silent and tense. Darcy had those pitying eyes that enraged Carly and she was too angry to trust herself to say anything. So, she reverted to her old ways of using her headphones as a way to repel unwanted conversations and she made a point of avoiding Jill during homeroom.

By the time lunch rolled around, Carly and Kim met up at the girls' locker room. They decided that would be a good way to target only girls with their first round of flyers. Carly and Kim had spent their tutorial periods in the library copying flyers. The flyers shared the bare-bone basics of how Kyle assaulted his victims, they had carefully left out their own names and ended with a warning that all girls be careful not to be alone with him or any of the football players listed below since these guys knew and supported criminals like Kyle. It asked any girl who was a victim to be brave and make a statement with the police to report the crime in the hopes that they would finally get justice for all of his victims.

After hastily stuffing flyers into every locker, they decided to meet up after school to use the rest of the flyers and post them all over the school.

When the final bell rang to dismiss the students, Carly called Darcy to let her know it would be another fifteen to twenty minutes before she could drive her home.

"OK. Well, Jill is here with me. Hold on a sec, and I'll see if I can get a ride with her today," Darcy replied.

Carly felt a twinge of guilt that she was putting Darcy out, but her mission was too critical to abandon now.

"OK, great. I am happy to take you home. I just need to stay a little late today. So, if things don't work out with Jill, I'll meet you by my car."

After a brief pause, Darcy said, "Jill said she can give me a ride. I'll talk to you later. Bye."

Carly had the nagging feeling that Darcy was annoyed with her, but she couldn't think about that now. Besides, if anyone should feel angry, it should be her. Darcy knew what she went through and how important it was for her to seek justice finally. She was supposed to be her best friend, and she, of all people, should have understood.

When Carly finally met Kim in the agreed upon hallway, they walked down to the first locker and began their work. Kim stuffed their flyer into the small slats of the lockers, and Carly taped some up every few lockers. They were determined to bring attention to what happened to prevent Kyle from hurting anyone else and also to see if there were more recent victims who might be encouraged to come forward.

As they reached another row of lockers, Carly began taping flyers to the front of them but noticed that Kim hung back, fidgeting nervously.

"What's wrong?" Carly asked, noticing her friend's hesitation.

Kim hesitated for a moment before speaking. "I don't know if I can do this," her voice was shaky. "What if people find out it was me? What if Kyle comes after me?"

Carly took a step closer to Kim, her tone gentle but firm. "You don't have to be scared, Kim. We're doing the right thing by speaking out and making sure he can't hurt anyone else. Besides, Principal Heathers said he would expel anyone who persisted in harassing us after we gave him the police report and our statements of what the other guys participated in, and we did that this morning. Kyle is going to go to jail, and his pathetic followers aren't going to get away with their harassment ever again."

Kim looked at Carly, taking in a deep breath. "I just don't want to be known as the girl who was violated... As the broken girl."

"You're not just 'the girl who was violated'," Carly said firmly. "You're a survivor, and you're strong for coming forward and telling the truth. We're in this together."

Kim nodded and gave a small smile of gratitude. Together, they resumed their work of slipping the flyers into the lockers. When they had finished with the last hall of lockers, Kim's older cousin, Justin, suddenly appeared in the hallway. He strode over to her, a look of anger on his face, and pulled her aside.

Carly watched from a distance, unable to hear what Justin was saying to Kim. But she could see the tears streaming down Kim's face, and she knew that whatever he was saying was causing her friend great distress.

After a few minutes, Kim's cousin stormed off, and Kim returned to Carly, still crying.

"Kim, what happened?" Carly asked, concern in her voice. "What did your cousin say to you?"

Kim shook her head, her voice trembling, "He's mad at me for posting the flyers. He says it will bring shame to our family and could even draw police attention to his mother, who is an illegal immigrant."

Carly gasped in shock. "That's not fair. You did the right thing by speaking out about what happened to you. You deserve to have your voice heard and receive justice!" she yelled.

Kim looked at Carly, her eyes filled with tears. "I can't do this anymore, Carly. I can't face the consequences of speaking out. I'm sorry, but I can't help you anymore."

And with that, Kim turned and ran down the hallway, leaving Carly behind. Carly felt dumbstruck as to what should be done now. Kim and Carly had both chosen to keep their names off the flyers. Aside from principal Heathers and the police, no one else would know it was them, would they? Carly wondered if the police would even bother checking into Kim's extended family. Justin was acting unreasonable and clearly didn't care that his cousin had been hurt. He didn't seem to care about anyone beyond his immediate family.

Carly left school that day feeling depressed. She had risked it all, embarrassed herself to make the police report, and posted what Kyle did to her publicly so that she could make sure he never got the chance to hurt another girl ever again, and yet when she got home, all she felt was depressed and alone. She kept replaying the scene between Kim and her cousin in her mind. Watching Kim walk away from their justice made her realize that no one cared as much as her. It made her realize that she was the only one who was ever going to care about the trauma she had endured.

By the time she had gotten home, she was in no mood to hurry through her schoolwork and eat dinner so she could get to work by 5:30 p.m. *Daniel!* The thought hit her like a bolt of lightning. She had been so laser-focused on ensuring Kyle got what he deserved that she had completely forgotten to return any of Daniel's calls over the past couple of days. She was supposed to meet him at work this evening, but all she felt like doing was grabbing some ice cream and curling up in her bed.

Carly picked up her phone to check her messages. She had just one new message from Daniel: "Hey Carly, it's Daniel again. Uh, I don't want to keep bothering you, but I just haven't heard back from you regarding our plans for this evening, and I hate feeling left in the dark. I'm going to assume you've had a change of heart, and I just wanted to let you know that I can take a hint, so I won't be there tonight. K bye."

Carly's heart sank. The only good thing she had going in her life was this budding relationship with Daniel. Yet it was over before it ever got the chance to really begin. She should have called him back and tried to explain, but the raw emotions of the past few days had made talking to him or texting him back feel impossible. Disappointment over Daniel giving up on her left her too depressed and bitter for words. She went to her freezer, pulled out the Hagen Daas chocolate ice cream, and went to curl up in her blankets in bed.

Carly cried and ate ice cream for a long time when she heard her phone ringing. She didn't want to answer, but she knew she didn't want to miss a call from Daniel or the police so she willed herself to the phone.

"Hello?" Carly's shaking voice uttered.

"Carly, where are you?!" came Heidi's irritable tone.

"What? I'm at home, why?" Carly replied sulkily.

"Jessica called to let me know you didn't answer the door or show up for work. You were supposed to drive the van there with the supplies and office keys. Now, I have a crew of cleaners on the clock, and no one is doing any work. Get over there NOW!" Heidi was livid as she shouted at Carly over the phone.

"Mom, I've had a really hard day. I can't go in to work tonight. Can't you get Jessica to come back and get the van?" Carly whined back. It seemed unfair that she would be expected to suck up all of the heartache of the day and go scrub toilets. *Why does no one care about my misery? Why is my mother so unfeeling?*

"Carly Anne Morales, you get your self-pitying lazy butt up off your bed and to those offices in the next thirty minutes, or God help you, you'll be sorry," Heidi screamed before hanging up.

Carly knew when her mother used her full name, she meant business. Angrily, she got up, threw on her work uniform, and drove to the offices. She wept the entire time, feeling the ache of pain lingering from the year of bullying and abuse, the embarrassing constant questioning from the police, the glimmer of hope that she could bring Kyle to justice, only to have Kim back out, losing Daniel because she was fighting for what she believed in, to having a mother who cared more about her precious business and profit margins than she did about the welfare of her own daughter. It was all just too much.

As she got to the offices, she saw that her mother had also just arrived. As the team started pulling out the supplies they needed from the van, Heidi pulled Carly aside. "What is wrong with you this week?!" she demanded. "You would think that finally resolving this whole boy issue would make you feel better, but not you. You just let it make you feel worse! You have one chance, Carly; you get in there and work hard or you're fired," Heidi hissed.

Carly felt shock course through her when she saw the stern anger in her mother's eyes, and heard the fierce reprimand of her words. She looked away to give herself a moment to try and shield her raw emotions and saw the awkward side glances of the crew as they slowly pulled out their supplies. She battled with every fiber of her being to suppress the urge to scream, to rage, to crumble under the weight of her emotions and her mother's heartless loathing.

For a moment Heidi looked into Carly's tear-brimmed eyes and seemed to soften. "I'm not trying to be cruel. But I know what wallowing in your own misery gets you. You deserve better than that. Time to put your big girl pants on and get back to living your life." Her icy tone told Carly there would be no sympathy if she gave into her tears or rage.

She nodded her head to show she had heard her mother and then turned to get to work. Carly did her best to focus on the cleaning tasks at hand. Every time she thought about how her mother had never once been tender and sympathetic to her grief or struggles, she began to shake in impotent rage. It made her furious that all of her life this had been how her mother responded to her emotions. When she was scared, her mother told her to be logical. When she was heartbroken, her mother told her, *"That's just what boys do."* She had never once felt the warm empathy she craved from her mother, and now when Carly felt as though she might never recover from the soul wreckage she was suffocating in, her mother was just as heartless and compassionless as ever.

At that moment, it was clear to Carly that no one would ever care about her, no one would fight for her, let alone with her. She was utterly alone in this world, and the only person she could depend on was herself. She vowed to herself that she would never let herself need anyone ever again. She promised herself that she would work as much as possible so that when she graduated, she could put herself through college and never have to live with her mom or ever depend on anyone again.

When Carly went to the private offices section of the building, she dreaded she might have to also see Daniel. *What if he did stay late and she had to face him on this horrible day?* She wanted things to work out with him, but she didn't know how she could ever explain why she hadn't called him back.

When she ventured to his office to see if he was there, all she found was a note that read, *"Carly, I think you are an amazing girl, and I really enjoyed getting to know you this past week. I'm sorry things didn't work out. Hope you enjoy your last year of high school. I wish you all the best. -Daniel."*

Carly ripped up the note and threw it in the trash. She wanted to sit down and sob that the one good thing she had going in her life had been stolen from her, but her puffy eyes had done all their crying earlier that day. She found all she had left was bitter cynicism. She hated that all men were either flakes, weak, or villains. The wounds from all the men she had known had left her too broken for Daniel, and now she would be alone for the rest of her life. Her mother was right. *Men don't care.* Jessica was right. *Men just use women. They don't have feelings!* Daniel had barely even tried. He just gave up on her after three missed calls and a few unanswered texts!

That shift went the quickest Carly's team had ever gone. She was quick about her work, and her short temper kept the other ladies hustling as well.

When Carly got home that night, Heidi was sitting in the kitchen waiting up for her.

"How are you?" Heidi asked tenuously.

"Fine," Carly replied brusquely.

"Good." Heidi sighed. "I just wanted to make sure that you knew I was here for you. I know you have been dealing with a lot this week."

"Oh no, I understand, Mom. Now that your business is secure, you have a moment to think about *my* feelings. Oh, I get it. Don't worry! I'm fine. And as soon as I can, I will be out of your hair and business. So don't bother pretending to worry about me!" Carly accused before she stormed to her room and slammed the door shut.

Carly's outburst of accusations was uncharacteristic of her, but she couldn't hold back anymore. She had always worked so hard to stay on her mom's good side so she wouldn't have to move back in with her father, Nick, and step-mom. But something inside her snapped and she found that she no longer cared if her mom sent her away. She would care about her mom's feelings as much as her mother had cared about hers. She hated that she felt she had to constantly earn her keep and prove her worth in order for her parents to love her or want her. *"Why can't they just love me for me? Why am I not enough?"* As anger finally gave way to grief, Carly cried herself to sleep.

The next morning as Carly arrived to her homeroom class just before the bell rang out, Mr. Rodriguez handed her a note from Principal Heathers, summoning her to his office. Carly's heart beat fast as she walked to his office, wondering what he had to tell her. When she arrived, she found that Kim Woodhall had also been summoned and was sitting in one of the two chairs that were opposite of Principal Heather's seat. The two girls sat across from him in silence as he finished typing something on his computer.

"You are probably both curious to hear an update from our last conversation. I am happy to say that I have spoken with several of the students who participated in your harassment and bullying, Carly.

Based on evidence found, and their own admissions, two of them no longer attend here and are now settling in at remediation school. As for the others, they have been made to understand that I will not tolerate harassment, bullying, or explicit comments being directed at other students. Failure to adhere to the stated behaviors detailed in our Student Conduct Handbook will result in their expulsion."

Carly looked over at Kim to see how she was taking the news, but her eyes were fixed on her shoes.

He cleared his throat and continued. "I was recently made aware of some mysterious flyers detailing the crimes Kyle committed as well as naming the same students who participated in Carly's harassment." He paused as he looked intently at Carly and Kim before going on.

"The contents of these flyers bear an eerie similarity to the statements you submitted to me. I wanted to take this time to remind you both that our school policy does not allow the distribution of flyers under any circumstances aside from running for class office and promoting an approved school club. Failure to follow school policies will be met with the stated consequences in our Student Conduct Handbook. In this case, a one-day in-school suspension."

Kim had looked up in shock at the mention of being punished for distributing flyers. Principal Heathers looked intently at Carly and Kim for a moment.

"As most people are unaware that these flyers state the same details as the statements you made for the police reports, I will leave you both with an official warning. You may not distribute any more of these flyers on school premises without consequences ensuing. Have I made myself clear?"

Carly was too upset and stunned for words, so she nodded her head and saw that Kim was doing the same.

"Unless you have any questions, that will be all," he said as he waved them to the door.

As Carly grabbed her bag and hastily left the room, she could feel the heat in her face and the pounding in her chest. Rage coursed through her and she wanted to scream. As she walked to her class the weight of the injustice threatened to crush her. *No one cares, and no one ever will. Why bother trying? Why bother fighting? It'll only get you into more trouble.*

By the time she was back in class Carly had promised herself that she would never talk to anyone about what Kyle had done. She would never bring it up again. She would stuff down her hurts until they were buried so deep, that even she couldn't find them.

Chapter 9: Prom Party

Carly had made up her mind that she was done trying to look cute, she was done trying to date, and she was done caring what anyone thought about her. Over the next several months she wore her usual gray and black hoodies, listened to her music, and avoided everyone except for Jill and Darcy. She still ate with them at the blue benches, but she was not the same. While they excitedly chatted about the upcoming Prom dance and who their dates might be, she just listened and agreed. She had no plans of going, not that anyone would bother to ask her anyway. She was tainted goods in all the boys' eyes. As the football team had put it, "She was the skank who got their friends expelled because she was a liar." All of it was nonsensical, but teenagers didn't care about logic; they had all made up their minds about her, and nothing she did was ever going to change it.

As Prom neared, Jill and Darcy asked if Carly would go with them. They tried to tell her it would be fun being each other's dates and that they would be "a cool trio of hot girls." Carly had thought about it for a while. She wanted to be happy and to enjoy Prom like a normal senior, but she knew if she went, she would inevitably be taunted by some loser jock or haunted by her memories of going to Prom with Ryan, and she would rather skip Prom all together than suffer through that pain.

"Please, Carly, it's my senior Prom, and you are my best friend; I want to celebrate it with you!" Darcy had begged, but Carly's heart remained encased in concrete. She refused to allow herself to feel much of anything these days.

"Darc, you know I love you. But I am never going to make Prom fun. I just don't have it in me anymore to enjoy school dances. You should go with Josh. He's cute and he thinks the world of you, and I know he's asked you a few times already. Just say 'yes!'"

"How did you know Josh asked me?" Darcy asked her brown eyes wide in wonder.

Carly gave a light chuckle. "Darc, we live on the same street. I saw his bedecked car asking you to the Prom."

Darcy tapped her nose knowingly. Will you at least come to Jill's house for the after-party? Jill is only going to invite a few of our trustworthy friends. No one there will ruin things for you, and then we can still enjoy our senior Prom together!" Darcy said hopefully.

"I'll think about it," Carly replied.

Carly had no intention of going to the after-party, but she didn't want to fight Darcy about this as well. She felt like her gloom was a wet blanket that she didn't want to spread. She couldn't escape her depression and internal rage, but that didn't mean she had to ruin fun events for the few friends she still had.

At school later that day, Jill was eager to ask Carly to the same after-party. It wasn't the first time she had asked her, but Carly felt certain that she and Darcy were in cahoots about this.

"Please come to the after-party Carly! No one from school besides Darcy, Josh, and you are even invited. Everyone there is part of my youth group at church. Even if they knew the rumors about you, which they don't, none of them would ever dare act like how those vile losers have treated you."

Carly had met a few of Jill's friends from church once before when she attended a midweek high school program with her shortly after the Kyle fiasco. They were all nice enough, but they made her feel tainted, impure, and like she might contaminate them. While they were busy asking for prayer with "impure thoughts" or "giving attitude to their parents," she was hiding the fact that she had chosen to sleep with her boyfriend, had been plastered all over the internet without her knowledge or consent, and was labeled "the high school whore." The fact that everyone there treated her like she was one of them, a good girl with minor problems, made her skin crawl and gave her a sort of panicky feeling that made her want to run away.

"I don't know, Jill. Your church friends are all great, but I am just not a fun person. I don't think I could even pretend anymore," Carly said flatly.

"Don't say that!" Jill reached over and unexpectedly squeezed Carly's hand. "You may not be all sunshine and rainbows, but we love you just as you are. You don't have to try to be peppy or upbeat, just come and be yourself," Jill said in a passionate whisper.

Carly raised an eyebrow. She knew that Jill chose to be her friend and stay loyal to her no matter what, but the idea of unleashing all the storm raging inside her, to come to a party and be who she really was, was ludicrous. Jill could never imagine the depths of her torment, and she was too pure and innocent to understand how silly her invitation sounded.

"I'll think about it," Carly said after a long pause. Carly could see that Jill seemed to be wrestling with herself. After opening her mouth to speak, only to shut it abruptly right after, Jill finally turned towards her desk and began doing some reading for one of her classes.

A few short weeks later, Prom rolled around. Jill was going with Eric, a tall, dark and handsome guy from her church youth group, and Darcy had accepted Josh's invitation to go to Prom with him.

Carly made a point of going over to Jill's house the afternoon of Prom to help her two best friends get ready. She was good at doing makeup and wanted to try and "create memories" as Darcy had put it. Carly hoped that drinking sodas and helping her friends get ready for their first Prom would make her feel less broken, depressed, and angry. Instead, she found that being around her friends who could never understand how twisted up she felt, made her feel like there was a world of lighthearted goodness she would never be able to reach. She listened to Darcy and Jill's animated conversation about the Prom theme and how they hoped their photos would turn out cute.

When the limo Jill's parents rented for the special night arrived, Carly felt the bile of jealousy rising in her. Why did good things happen to everyone around her but not her? Why could she never get justice for what Ryan had put her through? Why did Kyle get away with what he did and only get a slap on the wrist? One hundred hours of community service hardly seemed fair for the life sentence he had inflicted on her, Kim, and Naomi. Why did she have to have two parents who were both so self-absorbed that they never even bothered to think about what she needed? Her mom and dad had never even asked her if she was going to go to Prom. Her mom didn't even seem surprised that she wasn't going. They never tried to encourage her, or offer helpful advice; they just wanted her to deal with herself so that she wasn't a burden to them. Nick had been selfish since the day she was born, but her mother had been worse; her mother had kept a tally of all the ways she was indebted to her for life.

The haunted turn of her thoughts made it hard to keep the smile on her face as she waved goodbye to her two best friends. They represented what her life could have been if anyone had bothered to love or protect her. When the limo was out of sight Carly allowed herself to drop her fake smile and breathe deeply to keep from crying.

"Carly, would you like to stay and help us set up for the after-party? Lilly and I were going to dig into some ice cream and pizza while we watched a movie before we bothered doing any more decorating," Mrs. Goodmen said. She was a kind middle-aged woman, who aside from a few extra laugh lines and a little weight, looked like she could have been Jill's older sister. Jill's younger sister, Lilly, was only thirteen but she was one of the funniest people Carly had ever met. She had a unique way of seeing the world, and her ideas made everyone laugh.

"Aw, thanks, Mrs. Goodmen; I need to get back home. I didn't tell Darcy or Jill, but I won't be able to come tonight. If they notice, maybe you can let them know for me?" Carly said as cheerfully as she could summon.

"Oh! I'm certain they'll both notice. Jill has been talking about you being at the party all week. She feels terrible that she couldn't convince you to go to Prom with her, and this party was her hope of getting you to have one last enjoyable memory of high school." Mrs. Goodmen's face showed her concern.

Carly's heart sank. Hearing that Jill had thrown this party and curated the guest list carefully so that she would have a happy memory of high school was too much for her to handle. "I'm sorry. I just can't. I was broken too long ago and I don't know how to have fun anymore." Carly burst into tears at her blunt admission and ran from the room. She had to get home where she could hide on her bed, and no one would bother her or care about her. She had learned months ago that as long as she did a good job at work, her mother didn't care what she did.

Carly drove home in tears. Life had never felt more unfair than right now. Her thoughts were fixed on how broken her life had become. If she had parents who loved her like Jill's and Darcy's did, maybe she would be at Prom making fun memories. Perhaps she would still be dating Daniel. But she didn't! She had no one but herself to rely on, and she was just a weak teenage girl. She hadn't known enough about the world and boys to understand how to protect herself until the damage was already done. Why did her father only ever care about Shellie and Joey? He never cared about her except in her role as babysitter for her brother. He never even paid her to watch Joey, even though he knew she was trying to save up for a car and college. He paid his other babysitter $14 an hour, and she knew she was better with Joey than that college student. Her mother only seemed to care about her if she was disrupting her profit margins. She was just an asset. Carly felt certain that her parents only loved her for what she could do for them, not for who she was.

When she got home, the storm raging in her heart was pulling her deeper into a fit of depression that she had no desire to overcome. She blasted her favorite Alana Morrissett album, pulled her covers over her, and cried bitterly until she fell asleep.

It was dark outside when she heard her phone ringing. She reached across her bed to answer it. "Hello," she said faintly.

"Carly, get dressed because we are coming in there to get you. You aren't skipping out on our party! You hear me? Josh and Eric are waiting outside and will drag you out if we say so!" Carly shot up at Darcy's angry tone.

"What? Darcy, leave me alone. I don't want to go to some stupid Prom party!" Heart pounding, Carly hung up the phone and tried to hide under her covers again.

Suddenly, her bedroom window was thrust open, and Darcy, in a full-length Prom dress, awkwardly fumbled through. "Are you clothed?" she demanded angrily.

"Yes," Carly whispered.

"Good. You have five minutes to pull yourself together. You can go like that or you can freshen up and put on this dress," Darcy growled as she pulled her pink, floral sundress from Carly's closet and threw it on her bed.

"It's up to you how you come, but you will be coming! I've had enough of your pity party. You need to appreciate that you have friends who have gone through a lot of trouble to throw a party that you *will* enjoy. This party is just as much for you as it is for Jill and me!" Darcy was yelling, and Carly couldn't remember ever seeing her so angry.

In the span of fifteen minutes, Carly had thrown on some makeup, put the dress on, spritzed herself with an abundance of perfume and dry shampoo, and was grabbing her shoes to walk out the door. Even with only a few minutes to get ready, she was beautiful. Carly's dark brown wavy hair was twisted up in an elegant knot, and the smoky-eye look she had applied made her blue eyes dazzling. No one but the keenest observer would have ever been able to tell that she had covered over red eyes, that were slightly swollen from hours of crying.

After a short limo ride where Carly was thankful to find she was not required to answer any questions, they were back at the Goodmen's house. It took all of Carly's strength not to sink into a depression while at this party of happy, dancing, chatting teens. It seemed that her two friends had worked hard to create their own little version of a Prom just for her. She was overwhelmed by their love, yet felt that her past wounds were like a prison that she was trapped in wherever she went. She forced a fake smile on her face and did her best to act cheerful like everyone else.

When Jill and Darcy came over to the patio couch Carly had settled in, Carly immediately stood up and hugged them both.

"Thank you for doing all of this. It's really amazing. You guys really are the best!" Tears threatened to burst through, but Carly masked them.

Her friends tried to convince her to dance, but Carly said she was going to grab some pizza instead. Carly sat nibbling on her dinner observing everyone around her. She was struck by how nice everyone was. They were courteous to each other and inclusive. She was asked to join the dancing several times, not just by Darcy and Jill, but also by some of the other guys and girls there. Everyone seemed to want to make sure she was having a good time. Carly couldn't bring herself to want to dance. It took all of her energy just to pretend to be having a fun time so that she didn't let Jill and Darcy down.

"Do you mind if I sit with you?" Came the sweet voice of a beautiful girl.

"Oh sure," Carly said, remembering where she was.

"Are you having fun?" the girl asked.

"Yes. This is the most fun I've had in years," Carly answered truthfully.

"Me too! I'm Julia, but all my friends call me Jules." She held out her hand to shake Carly's.

"Hi Julia, I'm Carly," Carly replied as she took hold of Julia's hand.

"Well, now that we are introduced, you can call me Jules; I have a feeling we are going to be good friends," Jules said with a laugh.

Carly wondered at this strange, lighthearted, and beautiful girl in front of her. They had just met, and she knew nothing about her. Was she a liar or just naïve to think they would be good friends? While Carly was left speechless by the charismatic girl in front of her, a tall, handsome guy walked up.

"Jules, Mom called. We have to leave in ten minutes. She said she wants you home before midnight because you have to be at church early tomorrow to set up for youth group service."

He was about to turn and walk away when he locked eyes with Carly. "Oh, hi. Fun party, huh?" he said awkwardly.

"Yep. Jules and I were just saying how fun it is." Carly was beginning to feel suspicious that Jill and Darcy had forced everyone to ask her if she was "having fun" or to make sure she did. Why else would these two siblings be so caught up with her having "fun?"

Jules looked between Carly and her brother and let out an exasperated sigh.

"You two are the least fun people here if that is all you can think to say to each other. Carly, this is my older brother James. He's a serious college man and thinks this high school party is beneath him. James, this is my new friend Carly. She's Darcy's sulky friend who also didn't want to be here. There, now everyone knows everyone, and my job here is done." And just as abruptly as she sat down and introduced herself, she pushed James down in the chair next to Carly and left.

Carly felt heat rise to her cheeks as Jules walked away. She was mortified at being called "Darcy's sulky friend." It was true of course, but she didn't want any of these strangers to know.

She sat in silence, unsure how to recover from such an honest assessment of her character. She also had no desire to make small talk with a guy who clearly didn't want to be at this party any more than she did.

When Carly finally brought herself to look at Jules' older brother, she noticed that he seemed just as uncomfortable as she was and was busy studying his shoes. Carly wondered why he didn't just get up and leave.

After a few tense minutes of total silence between them, James looked up at Carly and said,

"Sorry about my sister's rudeness. She's a very blunt person, and while it's normally one of her better qualities, sometimes she can be a little ignorant of the irritation she causes by it." James gave a half-hearted smile before fixing his gaze back at his shoes.

Carly was dumbfounded that he felt the need to explain anything. She had dealt with so much worse in her life and no one had ever thought to apologize to her for it. James' strange behavior intrigued her and made her want to say something, but she didn't know what.

"Oh, uh. It's all good. No worries... Listen, you don't have to sit with me anymore. I promise my feelings won't be hurt if you want to leave. I was fine sitting alone before your sister joined me." Carly played with the empty plastic cup in her hands to help her look less fidgety and awkward.

"Your drink is empty. Can I grab you another one?" James asked abruptly.

Before Carly could catch the words that came falling out of her mouth she said, "Well, you are a strange one, aren't you?"

She laughed her hearty belly-laugh at her own rudeness, and it felt good to laugh. But when she looked over at James and found that he was walking away, her merriment ended just as abruptly as it had started.

Carly felt bad. Jules and James were the only two people she had really talked to all night aside from Jill and Darcy and they must think she was crazy or just mean. Was she?

Carly had the sudden urge to hide under the covers of her bed, and when she looked at her watch, she found that it was 11:30 p.m. She had done her due diligence and enjoyed the party for as long as she could. She just needed to figure out how she was going to get home.

Her friends had escorted her to the party in their limo, and now she was beginning to feel trapped.

As she walked inside, Carly found Mrs. Goodmen and asked her if there was any way she could get a ride home.

"My mom is most likely asleep by now, and I don't really want to walk," Carly explained.

"Oh, honey! Jill said you and Darcy were spending the night. I set up the guest room for you girls. I called your mom a few hours ago when the kids said they were going to get you, and I left a message telling her about the plans and giving her my number so she could call back if she had any concerns or questions."

Mrs. Goodman had one of those concerned but kindly faces on, and it made Carly's skin crawl. She felt like she was being pitied.

"I assume she never called you," Carly muttered knowingly.

"No, dear, she hasn't called."

"It's fine. Can I just go to the guest room now? I feel really tired and would like to lie down for a little bit." Carly tried to downplay the heavy depression that was dragging at her. She wasn't just tired, she was exhausted. She felt like if she didn't go to a private room to cry her heart out soon, she would burst then and there, and she hated the idea of having spectators to her misery.

Mrs. Goodmen nodded to Carly, and then led her upstairs to their guest room. The room contained two twin beds separated by night-stands. Carly noticed that Darcy had already put her stuff on the bed closest to the door. Carly was thankful she could have the back bed and wouldn't have to be noticed when Darcy came in later that night.

"There are toiletries and chocolates in the nightstand next to your bed. Please eat or use whatever you like." Mrs. Goodmen gave a moth-erly smile before leaving.

Carly didn't feel as though she had any appetite or cared about washing her face, but her curiosity to know what was in the nightstand made her go and open the drawer. Inside, she found her favorite types of chocolates, a really nice makeup-removing facial cleanser, some face cream, and a note written in Jill's neat handwriting.

"Carly, I had a feeling you would be the first to go to sleep tonight, so if you're reading this, it means I was right. We are all going to my church tomorrow morning at 10 a.m., and this is me begging you to come with us. I picked out an outfit I thought you would look nice in. It's in the closet. Please take a look and let me know if you will join us. I'm so thankful we got to celebrate our Prom night together and that in six short weeks, we will be graduating! This might sound strange coming from a teenager, but I'm really proud of you. I know the last few years have been hard, but through it all you have been strong and courageous. You're an amazing person, and I am so glad we're friends. Love Jill"

Carly was crying before she finished the letter. It was just another stark contrast between how her parents loved her and how these people loved her. When she opened the closet, Carly was surprised to find her own clothes on the hangers before her. She wasn't sure what she had expected to find, but she wasn't expecting Jill to have snuck out her clothes from her own closet. It was a lavender sundress with a gray cardigan sweater. She had worn the sundress a handful of times but never with a sweater. It looked like a proper church outfit made from her own wardrobe. She felt her knees buckle a little and went to lie down and cry on her bed. To her surprise, she found there was also a large bottle of water and a small pack of tissues on her nightstand. The Goodmens really had thought of everything and had cared enough about her to set this up. They loved her and wanted her, and it was more than she had ever felt from her own family before.

At last, fatigue and soul weariness overcame Carly, and in her party outfit, with her makeup still on, she fell fast asleep.

Carly woke up with a start in the morning. Darcy had set an alarm that was blaring its obnoxious siren as she snored lightly through it. Carly got up irritably to turn it off, muttering to herself about dumb alarms. When she saw the time, she noticed it was just a little past 8 a.m. She would need to shower if she was going to look presentable for Jill's church.

As Carly walked out of the room in search of Jill, she was met with a chipper, "Morning!" Carly rubbed her crusty eyes and looked in the direction of the exuberance. "Oh, morning, Jill. I was just looking for you." She mumbled through a yawn.

"I need to take a shower if I am going to go to church with you this morning. Can I use your shampoo and stuff?"

Jill's eyes sparkled. "So, you're coming then!?" she asked excitedly.

"If I can get ready in time. Can I also use your deodorant and makeup too?" Carly asked timidly.

"Oh, girl, you have a fresh deodorant in your nightstand, and I packed up as much of your makeup bag as I could in a hurry last night. So, whatever you don't have you can, of course, borrow from me. I just thought you would feel more comfortable having your usual stuff."

Jill's sneaky thoughtfulness touched Carly, and she felt the depression and despair seeping back into her bones. She felt a sudden tear escape the corner of her eye.

"I'm sorry! I hope you don't mind; you were in such a state last night that I didn't want to ask, but I also didn't want you to feel unprepared this morning. I'm sorry for going through your stuff without your permission," Jill said earnestly.

Carly wrapped Jill in a bear hug and then patted her arm. "Your thoughtfulness and generosity have just felt a little overwhelming because I'm not used to anyone caring that much about me. You did great, Jill. Thanks," Carly said as she looked her friend in the eyes reassuringly.

"Oh, I'm so glad! We love you, ya know? But, um... well, Carly, you stink. Go grab the toothbrush and toothpaste out of your nightstand, and I'll grab fresh towels and meet you at the bathroom."

Carly laughed an overly exaggerated breathy laugh in Jill's direction as Jill ducked away from her stinky morning breath with a laugh. Carly walked back to her room to grab the items she needed. She hadn't noticed last night that there were, in fact, drawers in her nightstand, and the bottom one had both a mini deodorant and a travel set with a toothbrush and toothpaste. Darcy was still snoring lightly on her bed and looked too deeply asleep for Carly to want to wake her. Carly grabbed her clothes and toiletries and headed to the bathroom.

After Carly had showered and gotten herself mostly ready, she headed downstairs, where a delicious smell came wafting from the kitchen. Carly was surprised to see the table set with a full breakfast of pancakes, bacon, eggs, roast veggies, and potatoes. Carly's own mother had never made a breakfast like this. She wondered how Mrs. Goodman would have had time for all this, but to her surprise, it wasn't just Mrs. Goodmen in the kitchen; Mr. Goodmen was in it as well, cleaning up the dishes. Carly saw the love between them and, more still, their enjoyment of each other. As she sat down to eat breakfast, she felt a knot of envy clench her.

Chapter 10: Church

After a surprisingly short time eating a feast of a breakfast, the entire Goodmen household became alive with action. The girls hurried upstairs to put the finishing touches on their hair and makeup. Jill's younger brother and sister rushed to the bathroom for their turns in the shower, and Mr. and Mrs. Goodmen finished cleaning the kitchen and gathering all the water bottles and Bibles that their family usually took with them to church.

In what felt like no time at all, the girls were packed in Jill's brand-new Nissan, and the rest of the Goodmen family were in their family's van.

When the girls arrived at Jill's church, Carly noticed that a lot of the same faces she saw at the Prom party were now coming up and greeting them. She also noticed that Darcy's parents were coming toward them. *Did Darcy and Jill go to the same church? How have I never realized this? When did that happen?* At that moment, Carly felt as if she didn't belong. How could she not know that her two best friends, her only friends, went to the same church? Self-hate began to creep up into her mind; thoughts of how worthless and dumb she was were beginning to consume her attention.

Carly was struggling to not completely shut down when Jim and Carol Campbell approached them and hugged each of them as if they were all their daughters, instead of just Darcy.

"Did you girls have fun last night?" Mrs. Campbell asked exuberantly. Carol Campbell was a thin elegant-looking woman and who always wore bright neon colors that made her chocolate skin tone glow. She was still holding onto Darcy in a side hug that made Carly wish her own mother enjoyed being around her like this.

As Darcy did most of the talking, retelling the events of the Prom and the after-party, Carly was spared from having to do any participating beyond the occasional nod, which gave her time to observe the fact that everyone here seemed to be happy. Everywhere she turned people were smiling and greeting each other with cheerful "hellos." The widespread cheerfulness made her uncomfortable. She had never been treated like this in her entire life. Were these people crazy, or was she just so far gone that she had no idea how to be happy anymore?

Right at 10 a.m. the entire throng of people who had been getting coffee and doughnuts and chatting happily all started to move to the recently opened sanctuary doors. Carly had just grabbed her own cup of coffee when someone bumped her and made her spill hot coffee over her hand.

"Ouch! Watch where you're going!" she yelled before she had time to mask her own natural response and act more like these happy church people.

"Oh, I'm sorry. Here, let me help." Carly looked up, and to her surprise, it was James. He handed her some napkins and asked if she was burned.

Carly assessed her hand and found it was just red from the heat and sting of the hot coffee, but didn't look truly burned. "No, I think I'll be OK. Sorry, I snapped at you. I think I might have been looking forward to drinking my coffee more than I realized." She hoped she sounded charming and that her joke would suffice, but James still looked serious at her.

"Wait just a moment, and I will get you another one. Did you just have cream in it? Did you add sugar?"

"Cream and two packets of sugar, please. Thanks," Carly said as she wiped the spilled coffee off her shoes and the floor.

When James came back, his sister Jules was with him. She ran up and gave Carly a hug, "Carly! You're here."

Her exuberance was hard not to be influenced by. Carly found herself smiling and looking just as happy as all the people she had just envied.

"Jules, it's good to see you again," Carly said, trying to match her excitement.

"Here is your coffee, Carly. Sorry, I spilled yours," James said quickly as he handed her the fresh cup.

"The worship is about to start. Are you ladies ready to head in?" James asked.

Carly looked around to find Jill and Darcy to see where they would be sitting and was upset to find that they were nowhere to be found.

"I think I'm supposed to sit with Jill and Darcy, but I don't know where they went. They left me." Carly's nerves were on edge, and she felt herself ready to cry.

"Oh, Carly, I'm sure they saved you a seat with them. I doubt they would have left you if we hadn't been talking to you." Jules said as she patted Carly's arm reassuringly.

Just then, Darcy and her younger siblings came up to grab another round of doughnuts and get Carly.

"Hey, we had to grab the good seats before they were all taken," Darcy said playfully.

Carly felt as though these church-going people all had a secret culture and jokes that she couldn't understand. She didn't know why that was funny to everyone. *Was this church like a concert? Why did they have to save good seats? Why was everyone happy? Why did this look like a family reunion?* She was left wondering while Darcy and her siblings led her to the front of the sanctuary to sit with them.

Just as she sat down, an older lady sitting behind her said, "Good morning. Is this your first time at our church?"

"Good morning. No, ma'am. I came once a year or two ago. I'm here visiting with my friends, the Goodmens and the Campbells." Carly pointed to her friends sitting in the row with her.

"Oh, good. I have known your friends, the Goodmens, for a long time now. You are with some of the finest people here," she said with a wink to Jill, who had turned to listen to the conversation.

"Yes, ma'am," Carly replied, not knowing what else to say.

"I think this will seem strange to you, but this morning, I felt the Lord prompting me to buy this Bible and journal from our church bookstore. Now I am seventy-three, and I don't have any need for these, but looking at you just now, I feel him telling me to give these to you," she said with a large, wrinkly smile as she held up the items for Carly to take.

Carly saw the beautiful yellow leather Bible and a matching journal and felt dumbfounded. She didn't know this lady and didn't want to accept a gift from a stranger. *What did she expect in return?*

"I'm sorry, I can't accept that. I don't have any way to repay you for these beautiful items," Carly said as she turned around quickly so she could end the conversation.

To her surprise, the little old woman stood up, leaned over her seat, and said, "These are from Jesus, honey. He gives gifts freely to all of us who can never hope to repay him. Think of this as his investment in you. He sees your worth, and wants you to know that you are loved, that you are not alone, and that you have never been alone." With that, she plopped the items on Carly's lap and sat back down.

Carly couldn't hold back the tears any longer. They poured down her cheeks, and she tried to at least be quiet as she used her gray sweater to wipe away her pent-up emotions. The morning's strangeness, coupled with her own resentment and bitterness at her lack of loving, protective parents had been too much emotion for her to hold back anymore. She didn't know what to say or how to respond.

At that moment, Jill and Darcy both had an arm around her while sitting with her as she held the yellow Bible and journal to her chest and wept as silently as she could. Jill looked back at the old woman who had given Carly the gifts and said, "Thanks, Mrs. Carlile. I think God really used you powerfully today, and I know Carly feels it."

Just then, worship music began to play, and Carly's crying was lost in a sea of singing people reaching up and praising God. Carly sat in her chair, silently crying the pain in her broken, aching heart. She noticed her new yellow journal had little flower outlines of daisies on it. She also noticed that it had a pen on the side with the same yellow and flower outlines.

Carly took up her pen and began to write what she was feeling. It was the first time in her life that she had ever done anything like this, and the more she wrote, the better she felt. By the time the music stopped and everyone sat back down, she had written her heartaches out on three pages of her journal, and though her hand cramped, her heart felt lighter. Just then, Carly looked up and noticed a middle-aged man stood behind the podium and was speaking.

"Have you ever felt as though life is just not fair? And that if there is a God, he must not be a loving God because if he were, then life would be free from sin, pain, and sadness?"

Before Carly knew it, she was nodding her head. That was exactly how she had felt.

"Or maybe you have felt that God was distant and that if he knew the real you, he wouldn't want anything to do with you? Today, we are going to look into the life of Christ, and the people he chose to be his disciples. We are going to look at the sinners Jesus chose to give a righteous mission to, the unjust shame he bore for our salvation, and the free gift of the Holy Spirit that is the result of his sacrifice."

Carly found herself hanging onto every word this man spoke. She had never known that Jesus associated with sinners or that he, like her, had been shamed by someone. She didn't know why, but everything in her felt like these words were the very air her soul had been desperately needing to breathe in order to survive.

"Please open your Bibles to Matthew 3:16 through 17," the preacher said.

Carly didn't know how to do that, she looked around bewildered and found that everyone else seemed to know just what page to turn to. Suddenly she felt Darcy grab her new Bible and flip it open for her.

"Matthew is the name of the book we are in and chapter 3 is shown here and these little numbers represent the verses. See?" Darcy whispered while pointing out the key details on Carly's Bible page.

"Thanks," Carly whispered.

The pastor read aloud: *"And when Jesus was baptized, immediately he went up from the water, and behold, the heavens were opened to him, and he saw the Spirit of God descending like a dove and coming to rest on him.; and behold, a voice from heaven said, 'This is my beloved Son, with whom I am well pleased.'* Now if we look just one chapter later, in chapter 4, verse 1 we see something truly interesting, it says, *Jesus was led up by the Spirit into the wilderness to be tempted by the devil.'"

Before Carly could find the verse in her new Bible, the pastor went on.

"Now why would this same dove-like Spirit of God proclaim his pleasure and love for Jesus and then lead Jesus to the wilderness to be tempted by the devil? If I didn't know the whole story," the pastor said as he held up his Bible. "I might be tempted to think God the Father and the Holy Spirit were being unfair to Jesus, making him go into the wilderness. It almost looks as if God the Father didn't really mean it when he proclaimed his love and pleasure in Jesus. But if we dig a little deeper, we will see the full picture."

"When we keep reading in chapter 4, we find that not only did Jesus have to face Satan's tempting, but he did it after he had fasted for forty days and was hungry. Before Jesus ever began his life of ministry or miracles, the very first thing he did was build his foundation by knowing who he was. God spoke his identity over him, *'my beloved son in whom I am well pleased,'* and then gave him the Holy Spirit to guide him where he needed to go. When Satan came, he thought Jesus would be an easy target because he was hungry and physically weak, but when we know our true identity, it fortifies us and enables us to stand up against the lies. Have you ever had a lie told about you?"

Carly found herself nodding and silently crying again.

"It hurts, doesn't it? But what hurts the most is when people you thought knew you, believe the lie. Jesus was going to live among some of the worst sinners in the Jewish culture, and the religious leaders were going to call him a lot of lies. They were going to proclaim him guilty upon association, so it was imperative that Jesus face the ultimate showdown of an identity attack and successfully overcome it before he ever faced the sinful people he would die to save."

Carly was lost in thought. She had never known that Jesus was mistreated and lied about. She had always thought Jesus was the son of God and lived a perfect life. She didn't know that he had faced problems like her. As Carly looked around at the people in the congregation, she noticed that everyone around her seemed to be taking notes as if they were in class, so she opened her brand-new journal and wrote down on next blank page:

"Jesus was lied about and mistreated. First by Satan, then by the religious people." She wasn't sure if that was what she was supposed to write, but it was what stood out the most in her mind. Jesus knew what it was like to be lied about and that made her want to know more about Jesus.

She resumed listening to the pastor as he said, "Just as Jesus was gaining in notoriety through his speeches and miraculous power, Jesus is faced by the fact that the ones he came to save only wanted what he could do for them. They didn't want a relationship with him, they only wanted his miracles and provision. We see this most clearly in John chapter 6 starting at verse 41."

Carly looked at Darcy to ask for help finding the spot in her Bible, and once again Darcy expertly flipped to the right page and pointed to the spot the pastor was reading from.

Carly read how Jesus had just performed a huge miracle of feeding five thousand people or more from just a little bit of food, and now these same people that witnessed the miracle were grumbling that Jesus was saying he was the bread of life that came down from Heaven.

The pastor quoted the first part of verse 42 to add emphasis. *"Is not this Jesus, the son of Joseph, whose father and mother we know?"* Even after his display of power, these people questioned Jesus' identity, and once again, just like in his wilderness training that we read about before, Jesus has to speak the truth and proclaim his true identity as the son of God. If we keep reading, we find that his identity and the message of his salvation was so offensive to many of the people who not one chapter earlier were thinking of taking him by force to be their leader, that they walked away from following Jesus."

"In John chapter 6, verse 60 it says, *'When many of his disciples heard it, they said, 'This is a hard saying; who can listen to it?'* and then in verse 66, after Jesus questions their motives, we find that *'After this many of his disciples turned back and no longer walked with him.'* These disciples were people Jesus had invested in, and they walked away from him because he openly proclaimed that he was the *'bread of life,'* which was another way of saying he was their Messiah. Now I don't know about you, but if you have ever had a friend that you loved, that you invested time into, and that you thought really valued you, just walk away from you, then you might understand a small piece of the heartbreak Jesus must have experienced when they rejected him."

Carly wrote down, *"Jesus was misunderstood by his own friends. They abandoned him when things got hard. Jesus knows what it's like to be betrayed and misunderstood."*

She stared at that sentence for a long time before she realized she was crying noisily. All of this time she had felt so alone in her pain and suffering. She had felt like she was the only one with parents who didn't pay attention to her or seem to care about her. Like she was the only one who had friends betray her or people she loved hurt her, but now she saw that Jesus had experienced the pain of betrayal and disloyalty. Jesus knew the sting of injustice just like she had, and more than anything she wanted to know how he overcame it all. *How did Jesus stop hurting? Did he get revenge on his enemies? Did he get justice on the friends that betrayed him?* As Carly wondered this, she realized that she hadn't been listening to the sermon and looked up to refocus on the pastor while wiping away tears and snot with her sleeve.

"After Jesus ascended into Heaven the disciples did as he said, they waited in prayer for the Holy Spirit to arrive. And boy did he."

Carly was getting ready to write down how the Holy Spirit got justice on all those who abused and killed Christ and mistreated him when the pastor continued.

"When the tongues of fire rested upon the disciples, they went out and immediately began preaching as we see in Acts chapter 2. Peter preaches the sermon of a lifetime that is meant to illuminate the truth of Jesus' identity and he finishes it by saying in verse 36, '*Let all of the house of Israel therefore know for certain that God has made him both Lord and Christ, this Jesus whom you crucified.*' It would be easy to assume that Peter would call down fire from Heaven to smite all of these religious men who killed their own savior, but God is merciful beyond measure as we will see. Verses 37 through 39 tell us how the Holy Spirit filled Peter with words of redemption: '*Now when they heard this, they were cut to the heart, and said to Peter and the rest of the apostles, 'Brothers, what shall we do?' And Peter said to them, 'Repent and be baptized every one of you in the name of Jesus Christ for the forgiveness of your sins, and you will receive the gift of the Holy Spirit. For the promise is for you and your children and for all who are far off, everyone whom the Lord our God calls to himself.*'"

"I don't know about you, but if I were facing a mob of men who had taken part in killing my friend, my savior, and my teacher, I don't think I would want to instruct them on how to join the club. But Peter was filled with God's Holy Spirit and was being led by him. He had to say what God wanted him to say. It's in these few verses that we see God's heart for sinners and the lost so clearly. The very same men who yelled "crucify him" were now being given the chance to repent of their past sins and be cleansed of them. They were invited into a holy union with their Creator-God, and all that they had to do was choose to walk away from their past sins and accept their new identity of being holy and set apart in Christ through baptism."

The pastor paused for a good long minute looking out at the congregation. "If there is anyone here who has not yet given their life to Jesus and received the power of the Holy Spirit in their heart, I invite you now to come down and repent and receive the cleansing and free gift of salvation."

Carly felt her heart pounding. She had not expected this. Her mind reeled. She knew everyone in her row was giving her side-eyed glances wondering if she was going to go forward, but she couldn't. She had too many questions and doubts. She needed more information. She wanted to be set free from her pain, her regrets, and her shame, but she had been let down so many times before; she had been bamboozled before and she couldn't just go down and make a fool of herself only to go back on her commitment the next day. Her heart was beating so hard she felt as though Darcy and Jill could hear it. Her palms felt sweaty, and her stomach was in knots. She turned and looked at Darcy who was sitting next to her. Darcy looked really excited as if she was going to give her a gift which only made Carly feel worse.

"I'm not ready. I have so many questions and doubts. I want to know more, but I am not ready to go down and give my life to someone I don't really know or understand." Carly buried her face in her hands.

But Darcy grabbed her hands from her face and looked into her eyes. "I understand Carly. We can learn more about Jesus together, and maybe one day soon you'll feel ready. No one is going to force you. It has to be entirely your decision and choice." Darcy's eyes were filled with gentle kindness and she gave Carly's hands a tight squeeze before letting go.

Just then the congregation erupted in cheers and clapping, Carly saw two young people walking to the front of the church to kneel before the large cross on the stage. A moment later, a balding, middle-aged man walked up as well, crying hard, as he too kneeled before the cross placed in front of the pulpit.

The pastor raised his hands to quiet the cheering celebration and said, "If you are a believer and feel comfortable doing so, please raise your hands toward these newly saved as we pray the sinner's prayer and ask God to protect and bless them.

He looked to the three on the stage kneeling at the cross and then kneeled with them. "For you three please repeat after me as I lead you in a simple prayer. This prayer is not a magic get-out-of-hell-free card. It is just the first step on your journey with Christ as you surrender to him and receive the power of the Holy Spirit. Repentance is the key that unlocks the gates of freedom. Now, repeat after me. *'Lord I repent. I have lived a sinful life, and I have made many mistakes. I ask you now to forgive me of my sins. I believe that Jesus died to save me from my sins and give me the gracious gift of salvation, and I want this cleansing freedom in my life. I invite your Holy Spirit into my heart as I surrender to Jesus and acknowledge that you alone are my Lord and Savior. Amen.'"*

At this moment the entire congregation got up on their feet and cheered and clapped ecstatically as the worship leaders played an up-beat song Carly didn't know.

As everyone around her was singing and clapping with joy, Carly felt sadness. She wanted the joy she saw on those three new Christians' faces. She wanted her sins and pain washed away. She wanted the comfort of the Holy Spirit. But she needed to be certain. She remembered her wounds, and she remembered why she couldn't just trust instantly, and knew she was just more far gone than those people on stage. Her heart sank.

Chapter 11: Transformation Begins

After church, no one said anything about her not giving her life to Jesus. They talked about the message, admired her new Bible and journal, talked about Mrs. Carlile's life, and lunch plans, but they never asked her why she didn't go down to get saved, and for that, Carly was thankful.

At lunch, Carly was surprised to see James and Jules' family at the same restaurant. Jules came over immediately to say hello and give the three girls hugs.

"Carly, are you busy this Wednesday night?" Jules asked cheerfully.

"Sorry, Jules. I work just about every night for my mom's business," Carly replied.

"Oh well, wouldn't your mom be understanding if you told her you needed to stop working on Wednesdays so you could go to a church youth group?" Jules asked hopefully.

Carly wanted to say, *"You really don't know my mom."* But she contented herself with, "I'm a manager in my mom's company, and it's pretty impossible for me to get any time off because my mom holds me to higher standards."

Jules frowned slightly. "Hmm. Well, I'm praying that God makes a way for you to come to our youth group. I think you would really enjoy it. We eat cookies, play games, sing songs, and learn how to follow Jesus. What's not to enjoy?" Jill and Darcy were both nodding their fervent agreement.

Carly wasn't sure how she felt about going to this youth group. She already felt like she was too different from the other church kids to blend in. Her life had been nothing like theirs, and the fact that she was constantly depressed or anxious made it harder to want to be around these happy kids who would never understand her pain. She didn't know how to respond to Jules saying she would pray. Carly felt certain that there was nothing and nobody that could convince her mom to give her Wednesdays off, and she wouldn't even bother asking. Carly had learned early on that her mother valued her business far more than Carly's happiness, and she didn't have the heart to try and compete anymore.

Carly just smiled back at Jules instead of trying to verbalize her family dynamic. After they had ordered their taco surf plates, they all sat down together. Carly found she was sitting next to James. She wanted to move away from him but couldn't do it without making a scene since Jill and Darcy had her boxed in on the other side. To Carly, James was strange. He didn't follow the normal socially acceptable patterns that Carly had thought he should, and his awkward way of responding to her made Carly feel even more awkward when she was near him.

"What did ya you think of the message today?" James asked before taking a large bit of his chicken fajita taco.

"It was really interesting," Carly mumbled as she, too, took a bite.

"What did you find interesting?" James asked through his mouthful of food.

Carly groaned inside. Any normal person would know that 'interesting' is just a polite word that means very little and would leave it alone, *Why is this guy so out of touch!?*

She thought for a long moment, chewing her food slowly. "I guess what I found the most interesting was everything he said about Jesus' life here on earth: like how hard and sad it was."

James nodded thoughtfully at her before taking another bite. Carly felt an impish impulse come over her. "And what about you? What did you find interesting?"

James smiled broadly. "I loved the whole thing. But I always feel like I relate the most to Jesus when I remember that he was abused, forsaken, and misunderstood. Like he really knows what it's like to suffer, and so when I'm suffering, I can bring it to him in prayer because he will understand me and is trustworthy to guide me through it."

"What do you know about suffering?" Carly blurted out incredulously before she had time to think about what she was saying. She immediately looked down and took a bite of her lunch to avoid seeing his response to her dismissive question.

James looked stunned. "It's not really a conversation for today, but if you don't believe that other people in the church have gone through suffering, you should stick around and get to know people more. Most people who go to church do it because it's the only place where we experience God's peace. I can tell you more about my life, but just not today... if you don't mind."

Carly felt too embarrassed and uncomfortable to make much of a reply. She nodded and mumbled, "Of course," before giving her whole attention to her lunch. The last twenty-four hours had made her entirely uncomfortable, and she felt as though her skin was crawling.

She wanted to go home, bury herself under her covers, and pretend like she didn't really exist.

At last, lunch was over, and Carly was sitting in the back of Jill's car, driving back to Jill's house to drop off Lily and collect her and Darcy's things so Jill could take them home. Jill blasted her Christian music, and Carly was thankful to have a reason to just be silent. She needed time to think about what she had heard and felt, and she didn't want to have to talk about it before she had had more time to reflect.

When Carly got home, she was relieved to find a note on the kitchen table from her mom saying she was out with friends and would be back around 6 p.m. Carly put the note back on the table and walked to her room and the comfort of her own bed. She had brought in her new Bible and journal, but was too tired and emotional to want to try and open them. She pulled her covers around herself and blasted some Indie Rock music to help soothe her to sleep. Carly found that the stress of the past twenty-four hours and the emotional toll it took on her allowed her to sleep most of the afternoon and night blissfully away.

On Monday, Carly was excited to find that she and the other seniors would need to line up in the quad to get their caps and gowns that they had ordered in the previous month. Carly hadn't wanted to part with the $89 for her cap and gown, but she was glad she did. This was an experience that missing out on would have only made her more sullen and bitter. She found herself feeling thankful that she was getting to share in the same ceremonial process with her two best friends. This bubbling feeling of gratitude felt new to her. She couldn't remember the last time she felt this light, joyful or excited.

As Carly and Darcy stood next to each other in line, she reached over and gave Darcy a long hug.

"Hey! Everything OK?" Darcy asked gently as Carly let go of embracing her.

Carly smiled broadly. "Yeah! Everything is great. I just wanted to tell you that I am so thankful for you. You have been like a ray of sunshine in my high school existence, and I am so glad I got to have your friendship through it all."

Darcy was visibly struck by Carly's new thankful and lighthearted attitude. "You look different today. Like you aren't carrying the weight of the world on your shoulders," she exclaimed.

"You know, I think all the sleep I got last night really helped lighten my mood today," Carly replied.

"Carly, you know I love you. I am always going to be here for you. But I have to ask. I know Jill told me not to, but I have to ask. Did you encounter Jesus?" Darcy searched Carly's eyes.

"I don't know. Yesterday was really overwhelming for me. I had a lot of emotions flaring up throughout the day. But this morning when I woke up, and I didn't feel that sense of impending doom -like my whole day was already ruined just because I woke up. I woke up, and my first thought was how pretty it looked to be outside. I don't know if I encountered Jesus, but today, I feel different... happier maybe."

"Whoa. Girl. That sounds like the miraculous work of Jesus to me," Darcy said seriously.

Just then, the bell rang out, signaling the start of the lunch period. As Darcy and Carly walked to the benches where they usually ate, they met up with Min and Jill.

"Did you guys try on your cap and gown yet?" Jill asked.

"Not yet," Darcy replied.

"I plan on trying it on at home. I don't want to pull it out here at school," Carly replied at the same time.

"We both went to the bathroom to try ours on," Min said excitedly.

"They are so long!" Jill exclaimed. "We will need to wear heels for sure, just so we don't trip on them."

As the girls ate their lunches and chatted excitedly about their upcoming graduation, Carly noticed she was just as excited as her friends, and for the first time in as long as she could remember, she didn't feel like an imposter. She hadn't once tried to manage her facial expressions or fake a laugh. She was genuinely just as happy to graduate as each of her friends. She couldn't remember a time in the last year when she didn't feel gloomy inside and wasn't putting on happiness like a mask to try and fit in with everyone else. Yet today, she felt so many beautiful emotions that she was actually enjoying her day.

When Carly got home, she went straight to her Bible and journal. She wanted more of the happiness and gratitude she had been experiencing, and she felt certain that reading the Bible would give her that. She opened the book to Genesis 1 and began reading.

Carly hadn't gotten more than two verses in when she read, *"And the Spirit of God was hovering over the face of the waters."* Carly's mind raced. *Was this another god?* she wondered before opening her journal to write down her questions. *"Who is the Spirit of God? Is he a third god? How many gods are there?"* Her questions felt silly to her, but she needed to know. Darcy only ever mentioned one God, and mostly, she had only talked about Jesus.

Carly read on to verse 26 and felt less stupid about her questions. *"Then God said, 'Let us make man in our image, after our likeness.'"*

She wrote in her Journal, *"Vs. 26 even says that there is more than one God, and he is talking to the other gods with him."*

She read on until she got to chapter 3, where the serpent lies to Eve about a fruit from the one tree God said not to eat from. Carly didn't like that part. She felt herself questioning whether God was really good or not. She wrote in her journal, *"Chapter 3: Why would God create a lying serpent? Why did God make a tree that Adam and Eve couldn't eat from? Is God manipulative?"*

Carly's mind was reeling with thoughts. She had barely read more than a couple of pages before feeling like she had to stop. She was going to need answers and hoped Darcy would be able to give them to her in the morning. Carly willed herself to put her Bible away and focus on her schoolwork before she had to head off to work.

The next morning, when Darcy and Carly began their drive to school, Carly could barely contain herself. She blurted out, "I started reading my Bible last night!"

"What?! That's awesome. What part did you read?" Darcy responded excitedly.

"What do you mean what did I read? I started at the beginning. I read Genesis; isn't that where you're supposed to start? At the beginning?"

Darcy chuckled. "With normal books, that is the normal way, but I guess with the Bible, it's different. Some people read the New Testament first. Some people like to start with the Psalms. It's really up to you where you start."

Carly didn't understand half of what Darcy had said. "I have questions about what I read. I have so many questions about the Bible. Can I ask you some?"

"Yeah! I would love to hear your questions, and I will do my best to answer them if I can," Darcy said as she positioned herself to look at Carly better while they talked.

"OK, so the first question I have that has been really bugging me is, how many gods do you believe in? I thought Christians only believed in one God, but when I was reading Genesis God was talking to other gods and said he would make humans like them. And this really confused me."

Darcy whistled. "Well, that is a good question with a complicated answer. We believe there is one God, who is three persons in one: God the Father, God the Son, and God the Holy Spirit. These are all different aspects of the one true God. It's called the Trinity."

"Darc, that doesn't make any sense. Does the God of the Bible have multiple personalities or something? Does he have three heads on one body? I just don't understand how he can be three persons in one." Carly was beginning to feel frustrated that her questions seemed only to produce more questions and not lead to concrete answers.

"I'm sorry, Carly. I think I need Pastor Dylan to explain it to you. He's the high school pastor at our church. If you came on Wednesday nights, you would have him and other leaders to talk to who are way better at explaining all of this than me."

"Darcy, you know I work on Wednesdays." Carly looked depressed. She knew she could never get out of her Wednesday shift as long as she was working for her mom, and as long as she wanted to live with her mother, she had to work for her. Carly felt like a prisoner and desperately wanted a way to escape but was hopeless that her mother would care enough about her wanting to go to church to let her "shirk her responsibilities," as she would put it.

"Carly, would you be OK if we prayed about it?" Darcy asked hesitantly.

"I don't know how. Could you do it?" Carly replied.

"Yes! OK, let's wait till we park, and then I can pray for us."

When the two girls arrived at the student parking lot, Carly felt almost out of breath with anticipation.

"So how do we do this?" she asked.

"Let's join hands. We bow our heads and close our eyes. This is to show that we are focused and reverent," Darcy replied as she grabbed both of Carly's hands.

"Dear Father-God, thank you that I get to pray with my best friend. Thank you for the work you have begun in Carly's heart. I ask, Lord, that you would allow her schedule to change on Wednesdays so that she would be able to come to the youth group Bible study. Please orchestrate this change, as we feel helpless to bring it about. Please bless and work in Heidi's heart, and please let her also want to come to church. In Jesus' name, we pray. Amen."

As Darcy said, "Amen," she immediately opened her eyes, and grabbed Carly into a hug. Carly made a mental note of Darcy's prayer. She liked how it started like a letter and ended the same way that the pastor had ended on Sunday with an "Amen." It gave her a framework to try and use when she started praying.

Just then, the first warning bell rang out. The girls looked at each other knowingly. They had exactly 6 minutes to make it to class.

"See you at lunch!" Darcy said as she began to run toward her homeroom.

Carly likewise began to run toward her class. She felt certain that if she ran through the courts, she would only need to walk briskly the rest of the way and would not arrive out of breath.

As predicted, Carly arrived in homeroom seconds before the final bell rang. She took her seat next to Jill.

Jill was her usual bubbly self. "Are you excited about Friday?" she asked with a giggle.

Carly looked at her perplexed. They weren't set to graduate for another month and a half.

Seeing Carly's clueless expression, Jill gave an exasperated "tsk" before saying, "It's Senior Ditch Day! We don't have to come to school that day if we are passing all of our classes, which we are!" She threw her hands up and said, "Woot, woot."

"So, you, me, and Darcy are going to get the heck out of here and spend the day at the beach!" Jill finished by giving a little happy wiggle dance in her seat.

"Oh wow! How did I forget about that?" Carly asked in amazement. This had been one of the lunch-time topics for the past two weeks. They had gone back and forth with what their plans should be and where they should meet up until they had finally agreed that Jill and Darcy would meet up at Carly's house, and the three of them would get together with a few of Jill and Darcy's church friends at the beach. The plan was to get tan, play volleyball, and boogie board till their stomachs were rubbed raw, or at least that was how Jill had put it.

Jill giggled and rolled her eyes at Carly. "I guess you have had a lot on your mind lately," Jill offered.

"Actually, that reminds me. I started reading my Bible last night. You know, the one that Mrs. Carlile gave me."

Jill's eyebrows shot up, and her mouth formed a wide-open smile, but she said nothing. She wanted Carly to keep going.

"Well, I have a lot of questions that I started asking Darcy. She tried to answer them, but that only made me have more questions, so she and I prayed that my work schedule would somehow change and that I would be able to come on Wednesday nights." Carly finished her story quickly because Mr. Rodrigues seemed to have homeroom business to address, and she was now the only one still talking.

When homeroom was over and the girls were walking to their first-period classes, Jill surprised Carly by pulling her into a big hug. "I have been praying for this moment for two years," she said through tear-filled eyes.

"All that time, you were pulling away from us and isolating yourself because of what was happening to you. All that time that Satan was taunting and harassing you through those guys, Darcy and I were praying. We wanted you to be whole and healed. We wanted Jesus to protect you from their lies and harm. We wanted you to feel like you did yesterday: light and happy. I will be praying for you to come on Wednesdays too." Jill said as she let go of Carly, and the two girls resumed walking to class.

Carly was dumbstruck. It had never occurred to her that her two best friends would be praying for her.

"Why didn't you ever tell me this before?" Carly asked.

Jill looked sympathetic. "We did. We used to tell you every day that we were praying, but you seemed angry. You would argue that prayer was meaningless and that if we really wanted to help you, we would tell everyone how vile Kyle was. But when I tried to tell the principal and the teachers, you got mad at me for interfering. At one point, we felt so bad that we stopped telling you we were praying. We tried starting the nickname Vile-Kyle, hoping it would catch on. Apparently, we just weren't popular enough for it to spread school-wide."

Just then, the one-minute warning bell rang out, and the girls were forced to part ways. "We'll talk at lunch." Jill had shouted from over her shoulder as she took off running toward her class. Carly, too, started running to her class. Her mind was reeling, she was reliving those conversations, but instead of being the angry cynical Carly, she was a hopeful optimistic Carly who wished so desperately that she would have listened to her friends and not isolated herself in the girls' bathroom for months.

Shame and depression filled her for the next two classes, and she found herself wishing she could just go home. How could she face her two best friends, who had loved her through one of the worst seasons of her life and who she had repeatedly mistreated and pushed away?

When lunch finally came, Carly walked slowly to the blue benches where they always ate. Darcy and Jill were talking excitedly, and both looked up just as she was a few feet from them. To Carly's surprise, she was met with a giant group bear hug. This hug did much to push away the shame and guilt that had been nagging at her all morning.

Darcy was the first to let go, but as she looked into Carly's eyes, her face turned to one of worry. "What's wrong?" she asked.

"I was just understanding the past in a new light, and well, I didn't like it. All this time, I believed that I was the victim. That no one else suffered but me. I believed that you and Jill were incapable of really understanding me because your lives weren't a living nightmare. But now I see that I could have gotten through that season with the help of my best friends and that I didn't have to suffer alone. I was so consumed with my pain and bitter resentment that I even took it out on you guys. How can you hug me and love me after all that I put you through?" Carly began to sob. She had been holding back these emotions all morning, and could contain herself no longer.

Without words, Jill and Darcy both went and sat down next to Carly, each put an arm around her.

Darcy was the first to break the silence. "Carly, we love you. I'll be honest. It was so hard watching you pull away and feeling helpless to make things better for you. It was really hard to have you be mad at us when we laughed or tried to look at things on the bright side."

Carly sobbed at the recollection of her yelling at them one day because they were making fun of their goofy English teacher. Carly was in so much pain and despair that their jokes felt like a betrayal. It hadn't been long after that confrontation that she had begun to avoid them and hide.

Darcy squeezed Carly's shoulders and continued, "But we understood that you were going through a lot of pain, and that pain sometimes makes it hard to see the good intentions of the people who love you. We love you, and if I'm really being honest, I think Jesus loves you so much that he made it really easy for Jill and me not to be offended or too hurt by you."

Jill chimed in, "I feel this way about Jesus. He has had to forgive me for a lot. But Carly, he loves us so much he died for us. There are a lot of times when I feel like I have failed and messed up, and I wonder how he could still love me, but he does. It's his love that gives me an example of how to treat my friends. You might have made some bad choices, but Carly, you did the best you could at the time. You didn't know what you were doing, and I really don't think you were trying to be mean to us by pushing us away. It's unfair to judge yourself so harshly now because you know more."

Carly had been trying to control her tears while her friends spoke, but their love broke something inside her, and she couldn't control the sobbing. She hated that people would see her moment of weakness, but she couldn't just escape to the bathroom. She felt deep inside her that she had to learn to face people and not care how they may judge her for being vulnerable. But with Jill and Darcy comforting her and being with her, she felt somehow stronger: braver.

The three friends sat there in solace until the bell rang out, signaling the end of their lunch break.

Darcy was the first to break the silence. "I have a presentation next period, so I have to get going now. But Carly, I love you, and we can talk some more after school today." She gave Carly a parting squeeze before grabbing her backpack and walking off in the direction of her next class.

Jill, too, stood up and said, "I know it may not feel like it right now, but what is happening to you is a good thing. In fact, I would say your change of perspective and heart are nothing short of a miracle.

Please remember that, and don't let Satan try to make you go back to hiding in your fear and shame. I don't want to lose you again to the gloom." She gave Carly's shoulder a gentle squeeze, and then she slung her messenger bag over her shoulder and she, too, took off for class.

Carly wanted to keep sitting there, but knew she would only get into trouble if she did, so with a heavy sigh, she stood up, grabbed her backpack, and slowly walked to her next class.

Chapter 12: Hospital Confessions

That afternoon, Carly got home feeling emotionally drained. But oddly, she didn't feel the usual ache of outrage and bitterness; this time felt different somehow. It felt as if all of the envy, hostility, anger, resentment, loneliness, and hate that had been storing up inside her for the past few years had drained out of her. Her friends' words of love and forgiveness had seemed to act like a person unplugging an emotional bathtub, and she could feel them draining away. In a way, having these pent-up emotions drain away was a relief. Carly hated herself for being angry and resentful all of the time, especially when she didn't want to be. But doubt and fear nagged at the back of her mind, *Who am I if I don't have my armor of hate, vengeance, and resentment?*

Carly had just made herself a bowl of cereal when her phone rang.

"Hello," she said through a mouthful of Frosted Flakes.

"Carly, where are you?" Heidi's voice asked urgently with a note of fear.

Carly looked at the time; it was still a little over an hour before she had to be at work. "I'm at home," she replied confusedly.

"Oh, good. You're still home. I was afraid you might have left already."

"Hey, Mom. I was just eating something before I started getting ready for work. Is everything OK?"

Heidi didn't respond right away. She seemed to be trying to find the words. "It's your dad and Shellie. They were in a car accident and are in the hospital. Shellie is fine, and she is being released to go home and be with Joey, but honey, your dad is beaten up pretty badly. The other car hit directly into the driver's side and..." She paused to blow her nose and compose herself before delivering the final news to Carly.

"Well, what!?" Carly shouted anxiously.

"He's in critical condition, and we need you to come to the hospital right away."

Carly could hear a ringing in her ears, and her heart felt like it might jump out of her chest. She mechanically wrote down the address of the hospital and put on her shoes.

Before her mind caught up with her body and she realized just what was going on, she was already halfway to the hospital.

As she drove, Carly prayed. "God. Uh... Father-God, I, uh, know you don't know me, and I know I don't have any right to ask, but please let my dad live." Saying her fear out loud brought on the tears, but she continued in her desperate attempt at praying.

"Please let him recover and be alright. He hasn't been a good dad, but he's the only one I have, and despite it all, I love him... Amen." Carly wasn't sure if her words would do anything or if she was even allowed to ask for a miracle for her dad, but she didn't have time to think about the religious protocols just then.

Carly parked and ran into the hospital to the third floor, where the ICU was. She asked the woman at the receptionist's desk for her father's room number, got her visitor badge, and then just stood there.

Her feet felt as though they were glued to the floor. Her heart started beating wildly, and her hands were sweating.

The nurse at the receptionist's desk looked at her kindly. "It will be OK, sweetheart. If you can't face him right now and just need to sit for a bit, it will be OK." Carly's knees began to wobble slightly, and she nodded her head to the nurse before sitting on a long bench just opposite the desk.

Carly sat there trying to catch her breath.

"You look like maybe you need to eat something," the kind older nurse said. "When was the last time you ate?"

"It's been a weird day. I had a couple bites of cereal a little while ago, but I don't know if I ate anything else today. I can't remember." Carly began to feel lightheaded.

"Here, start by drinking this," the nurse said as she handed Carly a small can of soda. "This will get your blood sugar up, and then you can eat this." She also pulled out a beef jerky stick and handed it to Carly.

Carly nodded and mumbled her thanks before drinking the soda and nibbling the beef jerky.

In a few minutes, she felt better: less weak and lightheaded.

"You're looking better," the kind nurse remarked.

"I am feeling better, too. Thank you. That's never happened to me before," Carly said.

"It's not every day that you have to rush to the hospital," the nurse said as she filed a few folders away.

Just then, Carly was pulled back into reality and her father's injuries. She stood up quickly, swayed a little, sat back down, and said, "Whoa."

"Just try to go slow for a while. I may have gotten your blood sugar up and given you some protein to keep it up, but you still need a proper meal," the nurse said right before she answered the ringing phone.

Carly stood up slowly this time and carefully began walking to her father's room. She waved to the nurse and then turned the corner to the hallway where her father was.

She stood in front of room 351, willing herself to just go in. She wanted to see her father and know if he was OK, but she couldn't make her legs walk in.

"Carly, you made it!" She heard her mother say from behind her. "I came as soon as I could, too."

Heidi took Carly's hand, and the two of them walked into Nick's hospital room together.

Carly didn't know what she expected to see, but her father laying in a bed covered with bruises and small cuts with wires and machines hooked into him felt terrifying to witness. She had always had a turbulent relationship with her father. He was selfish, immature, and lacking compassion for the feelings of others, but he was her dad. At that moment, she realized that despite it all, she loved him and craved his approval. Now, here he was, lying in bed, looking close to death.

Carly began to cry again. She walked to his bedside and gently placed her hand on his. "Dad? It's me, Carly. Can you hear me?"

No response.

"I love you, Dad. I am going to pray to Jesus to heal you, OK? I have never done this in front of anyone before, and I'm not entirely sure I will do it right, but... well, I want to try."

Carly gave a quick glance at her mother whose surprise and shock were evident. Carly bowed her head, closed her eyes, and began praying.

"Dear Father-God, please heal my dad. Please restore him to full health quickly, and please don't let him die. I love him. Amen." Carly barely managed to say the last part of her prayer audibly. Her voice was choked with emotion.

When Carly looked up at her mom again, she could see the questions in her eyes. She knew her mother didn't really approve of religion, but Carly also knew that Jesus was the only person who had ever made her feel joyful, even when her circumstances didn't merit joy. She believed that Jesus was safe and that he cared, and she was desperate to try anything she could.

Just then, a nurse came in to check on Nick's vitals and to change out his catheter and medicine bags.

"How's he doing?" Heidi asked timidly.

"Well, it says that he has a collapsed lung, a few broken ribs, and a concussion. He is scheduled for surgery in an hour, so for now, we are just keeping him prepped and as comfortable as possible," the nurse said matter-of-factly.

"Is there anything else broken or wrong?" Carly asked.

"His chart said he has a broken ankle and a broken wrist. It looks like those were fairly minor, so they were able to set them and place him in casts immediately. He is pretty banged up, and of course, his lung is in serious condition, but he should respond well to surgery, and we believe, with time, he will recover nicely." The nurse gave Carly a reassuring smile before she left the room.

"I need to call Shellie. She was in such a state of shock and panic to be home to get Joey that I don't think she was thinking clearly or knows any of this." Heidi pulled out her cell phone and left the room to make her call.

Carly sat there alone with her dad. He had tubes coming out of his mouth, tubes coming out of his arms, and other places. Her strong and energetic dad lay there looking frail. She had heard once that people who were in a coma could still hear. Her dad's coma was medically induced, so he wouldn't have to be conscious and in pain while machines kept him breathing, but still.

"Dad, why didn't you stay with Mom after I was born? Why did you leave us? I've wanted to ask you these questions my whole life, but I was always so afraid that if I did anything to disappoint you or upset you, you would leave me again. All my life, I have been living in fear that people who know the real me will abandon me, be cruel to me, or just use me for their own pleasures. And all the guys I have ever known seem to prove that true. Is there something wrong with me? Did you leave Mom because of me? I think she blames me for ruining your relationship. She has never said it, but I can see it in her eyes sometimes. You don't even know how many times I wished I had never been born. Or how many times I wanted to die... I don't know why I am telling you any of this. I guess it just feels like you are close to death, and all I can think about is how I wish so badly that you wanted to stay with us, that being alive and being my dad was important to you. I love you, Dad. Please don't die. Please get better."

Just then, Heidi placed a hand on Carly's shoulder. She had tears in her eyes, but looked like she couldn't bring herself to say what she wanted to give voice to. They remained like that for some time; Carly holding her father's hand gently, and Heidi standing next to her, holding her shoulder, both crying silently.

In what felt like just a few moments later, Shellie and Joey came in. Joey was holding a dinosaur and a car and was making loud crashing noises, much to Shellie's dismay.

Carly got up, wiped her tears, and went to her stepmother to grab her brother from her.

"Joey, let's go play in the hallway. You can show me how fast your car is," Carly said cheerfully as she blew her nose into a tissue to get rid of the traces of crying from her face.

"My dinosaur ate my other car!" Joey said in his sweet four-year-old voice.

"Oh really!" Carly replied enthusiastically. "And have we tried to get it back yet?"

Carly wanted to make the hospital trip feel as light and easy as possible for her brother. It was painful enough to have their father in critical condition on the other side of the wall; she didn't want Joey to have to try and process all of the emotions; he was only four, after all. She wished Shellie had never brought him here, but she knew Shellie would have no other help today. Shellie wasn't a bad mother, but Carly wished she could bring herself to think about what Joey needed a little more rather than just what she wanted.

After playing with Joey's toys for several minutes, he finally asked what was on his mind. "Is Daddy dying?"

Carly looked into his sad little eyes.

"Mommy said Daddy is dying and that if I'm a good boy, maybe he can get better."

Carly's jaw dropped. What sort of thing had Shellie said to make Joey believe such a horrible lie?

She grabbed Joey and set him on her lap, hugging him close.

"Joey, Dad is injured because he got hit by a car. If he makes it, it's because God allows him to keep living, and the doctors are successful in keeping him stable. If he doesn't make it, it's because it is his time to go to Heaven and be with Jesus. I promise you that nothing you can say or do will change his fate. You are not a powerful enough superhero yet."

Joey began to cry in her arms. "I don't want Daddy to go to Heaven!" he yelled. "I want him to stay here!"

Carly began stroking Joey's beautiful, curly brown hair. "I know, buddy. I want Daddy to stay with us, too. Maybe we could say a prayer for Daddy and ask Jesus to let him get better?" she suggested.

"I don't know how," Joey whined.

"I'll start, and you just repeat after me, OK?" In the back of her mind, Carly, wondered at herself. She was praying over her dad and praying with her brother, when she had only learned about prayer that morning. She marveled at the timing of it all. She needed prayer. It made her feel like she was doing something important when she felt completely powerless. It was soothing to her, and maybe that was why she kept doing it.

After leading Joey in a simple prayer to ask for their dad to be healed, they decided to walk to the cafeteria to get cake if they could find it.

Before they left the hallway, Carly peeked her head into her father's room to let Shellie know. "I'm taking Joey to the cafeteria to get something to eat. Can we bring anything back for you two?" she asked.

Heidi shook her head, but Shellie looked up, tears running down her face, "I'll take a sandwich if they have one. It doesn't matter what's on it; I just need something to put in my stomach. I haven't eaten since this morning, and I feel rather poorly."

Carly made the trip to the cafeteria last as long as she could. She was silly and playful to help her little brother cope even though she wanted to cry. They grabbed a sandwich for Shellie and a muffin for Heidi, just in case she needed it, and walked back to the third floor where their father was.

When they got there, Nick was being removed from the room, and Carly felt her heart beat wildly in fear.

"What's happening?!" her words came out in a scratchy yell. "Where are you taking my dad!?"

Just then, Heidi came out of the room, "Carly, calm down. It's time for them to prep your dad for surgery. This is a good thing. They are going to fix his lung so he will be able to recover better." She wrapped her arm around Carly and began gently rubbing her arm.

Joey was crying again. "I want my daddy!" he kept yelling over and over.

Carly reached down to pick up her little brother and hold him. "I know, buddy. I want Daddy, too. But we have to be strong for Daddy. Can you do that?" she said.

Joey just buried his head into her shoulder and began to cry harder.

Where is Shellie! Carly thought as she walked into her father's room. Shellie wasn't there.

"Mom, where's Shellie?" Carly asked in a panic.

"She said she needed to go to the bathroom," Heidi said, looking at her watch. "That was a little over fifteen minutes ago. When they came to get your dad, I was too busy speaking with the doctors to notice how long it had been." Heidi looked alarmed.

"Mom, I need to go find Shellie. Can you hold Joey for me?" Carly asked as she began handing her crying brother to her mom.

Heidi looked visibly uncomfortable and was about to say "no" when Carly snapped. "This is not the time to be selfish. Look at Joey! He is terrified and needs his mother, but she is nowhere to be found. I can't deal with both Joey and Shellie at once, so I need you to step up and help. Otherwise, just leave!"

Carly couldn't believe she was yelling at her mother. Just a few months ago, this would have been a terrifying thing that could have gotten her kicked out and sent to live with Shellie and Nick again. But she was too angry, scared, and sad to care about a little thing like that right now. She needed to find Shellie and slap some sense into her.

Carly ran down the hall to the women's restroom. She began banging on the doors and shouting out Shellie's name.

Finally, she saw her. Shellie was sitting on the bathroom floor, sobbing hysterically. Relief filled Carly as she saw that Shellie looked fine other than being distraught.

Carly bent down, pulled her stepmother up, and gave her a long, tight hug.

Shellie was only thirteen years older than Carly. She was Nick's fourth wife, and the two had met when she was only twenty-four. Sometimes, Carly had felt like she was the older of the two because she frequently had to act like the adult.

"Shellie, I know this is difficult. No one blames you for being upset, but you have to pull yourself together and go comfort your son! Joey is really scared right now, and the only person helping him is my mother!" Carly looked into Shellie's tear-filled eyes.

"My mother is terrible at comforting a crying child. I should know; she raised me."

Shellie gave a small laugh as she sucked in a ragged breath. "I'm sorry, Carly. I know this is hard on you, too. I just feel like this is all my fault. I had a miscarriage, and we were driving back home from the doctor's office when we got hit by that car."

"Oh Shellie!" Carly said as her voice caught in her throat. "I didn't know!... I..."

"Please don't tell your mother. I don't need her looking at me more pathetically than she already does. I just needed you to know so you could understand why I can't be as strong as you right now. I just..." Carly gave Shellie another bear hug.

"It's OK, Shellie. We're family, and we are going to get through this together. I'll stay with you tonight and help out with Joey."

Shellie cried into Carly's shoulder as she held her stepdaughter. "You were always such a good girl. We never deserved your sweetness, Carly," she murmured.

When the two women emerged from the bathroom a few minutes later, "Heidi was wrestling an angry and crying Joey. "Stay. Here. Joey!" she yelled through gritted teeth.

"Thank you for your help, Heidi. I can take him now." Shellie said as she tried to quell her own crying.

"Mommy!" Joey screeched as he ran into her outstretched arms.

Carly took her mother aside and relayed her newly formed plan of staying with Shellie for a little while.

"Tsk. That woman should be able to manage her own child and not have to steal mine to get through a difficult time!" Heidi said irritably.

"Mom, not everyone can be as strong and tough as you. Shellie needs help with Joey, and I know taking care of your ex-husband's fourth wife's child is the last thing you feel like doing right now." Carly had tried to make it light and make a joke she thought her mom would chuckle at.

What she didn't expect was what Heidi said next. "Your father is in critical condition, and you are still trying to serve, still thinking about everyone else, still acting like a parent to his wife."

Carly was about to start objecting because she didn't like her mother's estimation of things when Heidi held up her hand. "I know. I know. They're your family. I just wanted a moment to marvel at the beautiful young woman you have become and the gentle and kind soul you possess." She pulled Carly in for a bear hug and whispered, "I love you so much, my girl."

Carly felt stunned. It had been a very long time since Heidi had said anything complimentary about her or to her, and it had been even longer since she had verbally said she loved her. Safe in her mother's hug, Carly began to weep. The day had been so long and confusing, and this moment felt like a soothing balm over her raw emotions.

They stood embracing in the hallway for some time until Shellie and Joey could be heard standing next to them.

When they let go of their embrace, Carly noticed that her mother had been crying with her.

Shellie broke in, "The nurse said the surgery is going well, but that he should be in there for another hour or so. It's getting late, and I need Joey to get home and go to sleep." She looked at Carly.

Carly knew what that look asked, and before Shellie or her mom could say anything, she said, "Shellie let's trade keys. I can take your car and Joey home and get him settled into bed, and you can drive back in my car after you know Dad is safely out of surgery."

Shellie hugged Carly and kissed her cheek, "You have always been such a gift to me. Thank you for your help and support. I know this is a painful time for you, and I just can't thank you enough."

Carly could hardly believe that both her mom and Shellie were singing her praises and telling her thanks. She couldn't remember the last time any of them had said anything kind about her.

You are being made new, she heard herself think. And then she immediately thought, *That's weird. I wonder where I came up with that?*

"Come on, Joey. You and I are going home for a super cool slumber party. We are going to watch TV until we fall asleep." She grinned at Joey before looking up at Shellie and giving her a wink.

This had been a long and hard day. Carly couldn't remember when she had cried more in a day. Her dad was expected to be OK after surgery, and his chances of making it were high, but the fact that he was in the ICU at all still left her feeling like a frightened child, and that made her try harder to keep Joey happy and oblivious. She didn't want him to feel as terrified and uncertain of the future as she felt.

When they got home, Carly noticed that the house was a mess. It looked as if Shellie hadn't cleaned in weeks. Trash and dishes were piled up in the kitchen, and the rest of the house looked just as neglected. Carly immediately got Joey ready for bed and read him a story, and by the time she was halfway done with the book, her little brother was asleep. She kissed his forehead, turned off the lamp, and walked out of his room. Carly felt as tired as Joey, but the house was a serious problem, and she didn't want Shellie to have to come home to this, not when she had lost her baby, and her husband was in critical care.

Carly had remembered to grab her backpack with her headphones in it before she left the hospital, so thankfully, she was able to blast her cleaning music playlist without the noise disturbing Joey's sleep. She put her headphones on and hit play as she began to clean.

By the time Shellie got home, it was close to midnight, and Carly was asleep on the couch. The house had been thoroughly cleaned except for a pile of laundry that Carly had been trying to fold before she fell asleep surrounded by folded clothes.

Chapter 13: Recovery

When Carly woke up, she noticed that all of the clothes had been gently placed in the laundry basket next to the couch, and a blanket had been placed over her. She was still wearing her headphones and had a crick in her neck from the weird angle she had fallen asleep in, but she was grateful for the blanket Shellie must have given her.

Carly got up and walked to the kitchen to make a pot of strong coffee. She felt the weight of yesterday hanging over her, and she felt more tired because of it. Once the coffee was started, she went to the bathroom to find herself an extra toothbrush and try to put herself together as much as she could. She had school that morning and wasn't sure if she would be able to go home at all before she had to be at school.

Carly looked in the mirror and saw her mascara had run down her face, her eyes were swollen from crying and she had a fresh pimple on her chin. *Great!* She thought irritably to herself.

She used some of Shellie's face wash and makeup to clean herself up and cover her pimple as best she could before school. She just needed to borrow a shirt from Shellie, so it wasn't so obvious that she hadn't gone home the night before.

When she went back into the kitchen, Carly found Shellie just starting to scramble eggs and toast a few Eggo waffles. She had already poured herself a cup of coffee and gotten dressed for the day.

"Morning," Shellie said before taking a gulp of her coffee. "I spoke with your mom, and she said she was going to call the school and let them know you wouldn't be able to attend for the rest of this week." She took another sip before going on. "I will be at the hospital all day and thought it would be easier if you and Joey just tried to have fun here or at the park." She handed Carly a few folded-up bills of cash.

Carly felt her stomach drop. "OK. Did my mom say if she still wants me to report to work the rest of this week?" Carly asked, trying to keep the bitterness out of her voice.

She felt the injustice of everything. While her father was lying in a hospital room in critical care, she was expected to just drop everything and play nanny to her little brother. She couldn't even show her own emotions because that would cause a fight between her and Shellie, and she didn't want Joey to suffer because Shellie was unstable.

"I didn't ask her. Sorry, Carly, I forgot you were working full-time for your mom. I have had a hard time remembering anything since the accident. I can call your mom back as soon as I am done making breakfast."

"It's fine," Carly said, trying to mask her irritability. "I'll call her myself."

Carly felt at war in herself. She wanted to be helpful to Shellie, and she loved spending time with her brother; she just hated that they didn't even bother to ask her if she wanted to skip school to play nanny before forcing it on her. It brought up all the memories and reasons why she stopped living with her dad and Shellie in the first place. She always felt like the Cinderella of the family; like she was tolerated because she was a useful babysitter and housecleaner. She wasn't loved like a daughter. She was just a free servant. She knew these thoughts wouldn't help her get through this difficult situation, so she tried pushing them down, but she still felt the resentment bubbling just under the surface.

"Hello," Heidi's voice sounded raspy, like she had just been woken up.

"Hey, Mom, sorry to wake you. I just needed to know if I have to work this week in addition to being the nanny while my dad is in critical care!" Carly hadn't meant to snap angrily at her mom, but there it was: her rage and anger bubbling to the surface.

"Carly! You don't have to take care of Joey. I didn't want you to go with Shellie at all. If you remember, that was your choice. You said she needed you and that you were happy to do that. I would never have agreed if you hadn't said that."

Carly felt foolish. She remembered that it was her choice. She had felt like it was what Jesus wanted last night. Why was she eaten up with anger and resentment this morning for doing something good? What was this feeling that was plaguing her?

"Sorry, Mom. I know; I guess I just didn't realize Shellie would go right back to arranging my life to be the super nanny without even asking me how I felt or what I thought. I'm sorry I shouted."

"Carly, should I call Shellie and tell her I changed my mind? That I want you in school to finish your Senior year strong?" Heidi's concern for Carly softened her anger and made her feel less taken for granted.

"No, it's fine. I have all A's, and I don't think any of my teachers have anything really crucial planned for this week... You still haven't answered my question about my working the rest of the week."

There was a short pause before Heidi said, "I'll call Jessica and let her know I need her to cover for you this week. You don't have to work for the rest of this week."

"Thanks, Mom. I appreciate that a lot. I feel like a lot of unprocessed emotions are bubbling up because of Dad's accident, and I don't think I would be much good at work this week anyway. I am going to come home for a little bit today to grab my stuff and some clothes for the next few days."

"Of course, honey. I will take care of your schedule. Just let me know by Sunday if you can work next week... I love you, Carly, and I am so proud of the amazing woman you have become."

At these affirming words, Carly began to cry. She couldn't hold back all of the hurt and overwhelming emotions any longer.

"Carly, I can come get you right now. I don't want you to feel like you have to be a servant or nanny. You are going through a hard time right now, and no one would blame you for needing space."

Carly subdued her sobbing enough to tell her mom, "Thanks, Mom. I love you too. I think I need to help Joey get through this. Shellie will just bring him to the hospital if I don't, and I don't want him to suffer any more than he has to."

After Carly and her mother said their goodbyes, she returned to the kitchen to talk things out with Shellie. Carly was in a better frame of mind this time.

"Hey, so my mom said I can skip work this week, too. Are you cool with me taking Joey to my house for a little bit so I can pack my stuff for this week?"

Carly knew that Shellie didn't like Joey spending any time with her mom, Heidi, so she quickly added, "My mom is leaving soon, so she won't be home when we stop by."

"OK, sure. I know you need to get your things, and I can't think of a better way than taking Joey with you. I think I will just keep driving your car, and you can take mine since Joey's car seat is in it, and it's just easier this way."

"OK. I just want to grab my hoodie before you take off."

"I'm going to call my friend Darcy right now so that I can explain everything to her. She'll be worried when I don't show up to drive her to school in a little bit."

Carly called Darcy's home line. "Hello," came Darcy's rushed voice.

"Oh good, you're still home. Listen, my dad is in the hospital, and I won't be at school the rest of this week, so I won't be able to drive you to school," Carly blurted out.

"Carly! Oh my gosh! Are you OK? Is your dad, OK? Do you need anything?" Darcy questioned.

Carly felt gratitude and appreciation that her friend's first concerns weren't how she would get to school on time, but were concerns over how she was. "I am taking care of my little brother today while my step-mom spends the day at the hospital with my dad. I don't feel like we really need anything, but I would love to hang out with you and Jill after school. I feel like I'm still in shock and could use the company."

"Hey! Tonight is youth group! Why don't you and your brother come?" Darcy exclaimed excitedly.

"Darc, Joey is four. I don't think the high school group is the place for him."

"No, Carly. That's not what I'm saying. Our church also holds classes for adults and younger kids on Wednesday nights. It's a whole family affair, not just the high school group. Joey could be registered for the preschoolers' room."

"I would have to check with Shellie first. It's her decision if she wants Joey out later tonight or not. I'll ask her and then call you back on your cell."

"Sounds like a plan. Jill and I will also be praying you guys can come tonight." Darcy replied before abruptly saying, "Oh, hey, listen. I gotta see if my dad can take me to school this morning on his way to work. Talk later." And with that, Darcy hung up the phone.

When Carly set her phone down, she had butterflies in her stomach. She had really been wanting to go to the high school group, and this felt like some strange and fortuitous way of being able to go. She told herself to stop being so eager. She would know if she could go soon enough, but in her heart, she said a little prayer that Shellie would say "yes."

Carly leaned casually against the kitchen counter as she introduced the idea to Shellie. "Hey, so my friend Darcy and her family go to church on Wednesday nights and she invited Joey and me to go with her. She said that Joey could go to the preschool class while she and I attend the high school Bible study. Do you think it would be OK if we went?" Carly looked up and saw shock in Shellie's face.

"Of course, we don't have to go if you aren't comfortable with it. I know it ends at 8 p.m. and that's Joey's bedtime. He would be out a bit late and if that's too much for him I totally understand." Carly added abruptly.

Just then, Shellie gave Carly a big hug. "I would love for you two to go to church together. Joey and I have been going to a church nearby for a couple of months now, and I am sure he would enjoy going with you."

Carly felt stunned. She had no idea that Shellie believed in Jesus. She felt like her life was changing so rapidly, and her understanding of who people were seemed to be wrong in so many ways that she wondered if she was just wrong about everyone and everything in her life.

"I didn't... I mean, I... Sounds good." Carly finally stammered out before immediately leaving the kitchen to call Darcy back to tell her the good news.

Once that was done, Carly grabbed her stuff out of her car, and noticed that her little yellow journal had a Bible verse embossed on the front cover. She hadn't noticed it until now. When she went back into the house with her few comfort items, she decided to take a moment to try and find the Bible verse. It was "Proverbs 3:5-6." Just as Carly was looking through the table of contents in the front of her Bible, Joey came in.

Carly closed her Bible before greeting him. "Hey, buddy."

Joey rubbed his eyes. "Where's my mommy?" he whined.

"She's in the bathroom right now. Do you want to come eat some breakfast with me?" Carly asked gently.

Joey nodded his head, and allowed Carly to take hold of his hand, and lead him to the kitchen table for breakfast.

Carly made a mental note of the verse on her journal and hoped she would find time to look it up later that day.

"After breakfast, I need to swing by my house, but I was thinking we could go to this really cool park after that. What do you think?" Carly asked.

"I love the park!" Joey screamed as he wiggled around and took a bite of his waffle.

As Carly got Joey ready for the day and tried her best to put on a cheerful face for Joey, she realized that she could make this time of their dad being in the ICU a time that Joey would remember as their fun days together, rather than the scary feeling of fear if their dad would ever be the same again.

As Shellie was helping Joey brush his teeth, Carly sat on the couch and prayed, "God, please heal my dad. Please help Joey and me to have a fun day together. Please help me be loving and kind today and remember why I chose to serve my family in the first place. Amen."

Carly texted Darcy, *"Hey, can you pray for me today? Struggling with everything going on. Can't wait to see you tonight"*

Then she and Joey got into Shellie's van to head to her house and then the park. There was a park not too far away from where Carly lived that had wild peacocks and a pony ride. Carly wanted to make this day feel like a vacation, and she had always loved going to this park when she was younger.

Joey's squeal of delight when they got to the park made Carly feel certain she had started the day off with the right place.

"Do you want to go find some peacocks?" Carly asked as she took hold of his hand.

"Yeah! Let's go hunt some peacocks!" Joey half-screamed, half-shouted. His excitement was making him jump up and down, and Carly had to keep a firm grip on his little squirmy hand.

"Peacock hunting," as Joey had put it, turned out to be them running through the park at every bird Joey saw. He didn't seem to care if it was a duck, pigeon, crow, or sparrow; in his mind, all of them were different types of peacocks.

Soon, they had sticks, and Joey was trying to poke the birds that didn't fly away fast enough; Carly watched his exuberance with contentment. He laughed each time the birds took flight, and Carly felt confident that he wasn't actually able to poke any of the birds, so no one was being hurt by his game.

Carly sat on a park bench, watching Joey run around throwing his stick and chasing birds; she dug into her backpack and pulled out her Bible and journal. She still wanted to know what that verse on her journal said, so she looked in the table of contents of her Bible until she found Proverbs and then carefully thumbed through the thin pages until she got to Proverbs three. The verses read, *"Trust in the Lord with all your heart, and do not lean on your own understanding. In all your ways acknowledge him, and he will make straight your paths."*

A tear slid down Carly's face as she closed her Bible. She didn't know why this verse had made her cry, but her life felt as jumbled as a bowl of spaghetti, and she wanted so desperately for God to make her life clear and the path she should take straight. The past few years had left her feeling like her life was doomed to be tragic and miserable forever, and yet when she read this book, she felt an inexplicable comfort.

Before she knew what she was doing, Carly found herself talking to this Lord, who said he would make her path straight. She whispered, "Thank you. Please direct my path today. I don't really know what I'm doing or if I'm doing the right thing, but I am trying, and that is more than I have done in the past. Lord, I don't want to only think about myself today. Let me be a good sister and daughter, and let this day somehow be good even though bad things are happening. Amen."

Carly marveled again at how easily she had taken up praying, even though just a few short days ago, she had never prayed before in her life, at least not on her own.

Just then, Joey tripped and fell, sending his stick flying and him sprawled on the grassy lawn. Carly set down her books and ran to get him.

"Joey, what happened?" she asked in alarm. Joey had dirt smudged on his nose and tears rolling down his eyes.

"I fell. The tree tripped me!" Joey cried out with angry tears.

Carly couldn't help but giggle a little at how clever and cute her brother was. A tree root sticking up out of the grass had indeed been the source of Joey's fall. She wiped his jeans off and kissed his little knees. It was close to 11 a.m., so Carly asked, "Should we get some ice cream to make it feel better?"

Joey's tears instantly ended as he excitedly jumped up and shouted, "Yes, yes, yes!"

Carly laughed. She had forgotten how energetic and lively her little brother was.

"Alright, let's get my backpack, and then we can walk to the ice cream stand." Carly held out her hand to hold Joey's, but he ran right past her and toward the bench where she had been sitting.

The ice cream stand wasn't too much further into the park, but Carly still broke out into a run to grab her stuff and catch up with Joey. The last thing she wanted was for him to get lost when they were supposed to be having a fun day to take their minds off their dad being in the hospital.

"Joey, stop running! Or I won't buy you ice cream," Carly yelled through panting breath.

That worked like magic, Carly thought to herself as she finally caught up with Joey, who had chosen to stand absolutely still after her threat of no ice cream.

"Joey, I know you're excited, but we have to stick together. You can't just run off when you want to, OK?"

"I was just going to the ice cream stand like you said," Joey replied defensively.

"I know, buddy, but I have to be with you while you go."

"You are with me," Joey replied in confusion.

Carly laughed. And muttered to herself, "Kids."

When ice cream was eaten, Joey began to ask if they could go and ride the horses. They had been sitting on a bench watching other young kids ride the ponies in a large circular corral with their parents walking alongside them. Now that Carly had popped the last bite of her cone into her mouth, Joey was like a broken record, just repeating over and over, "Can we ride the horses? Can we? Can we?"

With a mouth full of ice cream, Carly held up her hand to stop the constant stream of questions coming from her brother and to indicate that she planned on speaking as soon as her mouth wasn't full.

Finally, she replied, "OK, Joey, we can ride the horses, but just once. Your mom only gave me enough money for you to ride once. After that, we have to start walking back to the car so we can eat lunch at home. OK?"

"Yay, horses!! Let's go now!" Joey screamed excitedly.

Carly had the feeling that he wasn't going to get back to the car easily, so she whispered a quiet prayer; "God, please let this day be fun, but let my brother be cooperative and go back to the car easily. Amen."

The pony ride was $10 and lasted ten minutes. They had put a bandana around Joey's neck, and he kept hooting and hollering, "Yee-haw, I'm a cowboy," much to the delight of the adults around them. Joey's exuberance was so loud and noticeable that soon other kids were yelping "Yeehaw" as well.

Carly marveled at her little brother. He had the ability to walk into a place, captivate everyone's attention, and then get the other kids to copy him because he was having so much fun, and they wanted to be that joyful too. Suddenly, Carly found herself on the verge of tears again. She hoped that life would be kinder to Joey than it had been to her. Like maybe if her life wasn't so broken and marked by pain, she could have been this fun, exuberant, and influential. She found herself wishing that she had had an older sister to take her to the park and buy her ice cream so that she could have been as happy and carefree as Joey was.

By the time the ride was over, Carly was feeling bitter and angry that the adults in her life hadn't loved her enough to protect her or try to give her a happy life.

"I want to ride again!" Joey said as Carly reached up to take him off his pony.

"No, Joey, we talked about this; you only get to ride once," Carly snapped more angrily than she had meant to.

Joey began to cry, and suddenly, Carly was embarrassed by the number of eyes looking at them.

Joey was hysterical as Carly pulled him off the pony, and handed the bandana back to the employee, "No, I'm a cowboy! That's mine!" he screamed through tears.

And when it was clear he wasn't going to get his way, he plopped down into the dirt, sobbed, and began to flail about.

Carly could feel her own anger rising. She had worked so hard to make this day special for him and had spent their lunch money on ice cream, and a pony ride and this was how he thanked her!? She picked her screaming brother up off the ground, slung him over her shoulder, and began to march back to the car. She didn't care how many people looked at their noisy passing; she just kept marching on. Joey had taken to punching her on her backpack and trying to kick her stomach. Finally, his foot made contact, and she dropped him on the grass.

"What is wrong with you!?" she yelled angrily. "You don't get to hurt people just because you don't get every little thing you want! You're acting like a monster!" she screamed while clutching her stomach.

Joey began crying again. This time, his hysterical crying made him impossible to comprehend, but Carly thought she heard him say, "I'm sorry," mixed with the jumble of words she couldn't make out.

Carly was so angry at him, but she also knew she shouldn't try to hurt her brother just because he was throwing a tantrum and acting like a maniac. Carly scooted over to where Joey was sitting and put her arms around her crying brother.

"I love you, Joey; I forgive you." And she sat holding his little form as he buried his head into her and cried.

Finally, all worn out, Joey relaxed into just hugging her.

"Are you ready to go home and eat lunch?" Carly asked.

But when she looked down, Joey was asleep.

Carly carried a quiet and sleeping Joey to the car and buckled him into his seat. She reminded herself that he hadn't gotten very much sleep last night either and that they were both probably really hungry. He was just a little kid.

As she drove back to her dad's house, Carly prayed yet again. "God, please help me be a loving sister and to be kind to Joey today. Please heal my dad and help my family. Amen."

Carly couldn't fully understand why she was praying so much; she just knew it made her feel less anxious when she did.

Chapter 14: Youth Group

That afternoon, Carly was cleaning up the lunch dishes when her phone began to ring.

"Hey, Jill," Carly said as she used her shoulder to hold her phone to her ear.

"Hey, how are you doing? Darcy told me about your dad." Jill's voice sounded concerned.

"I'm alright. I have been taking care of my brother all day so that my step-mom can be at the hospital with my dad, and so that Joey can have a fun and peaceful day without worrying about our dad." Carly scrubbed the dishes as she spoke.

"What are you doing? It's so loud," Jill replied.

"Sorry, I was trying to clean up our lunch dishes and I had the water running. Is this better?" Carly asked as she turned the water off.

"Yes, thanks. I'm sorry your dad is in the hospital. Darcy and I prayed for him at lunch today."

"Thanks, Jill. I appreciate your prayers. Shellie called me earlier and said that the doctors said he should stabilize today and will probably be taken out of his coma by tomorrow morning," Carly said as she fought back emotion.

"We are praying he recovers quickly and fully. Uhm, well, hey, Darcy said you and your brother are coming to youth group tonight."

Carly noticed how Jill seemed to be struggling to find words to say to her.

"Yeah, Darcy said there is a kids' program for Joey that I can drop him off in, and then I can attend the high school group. Kinda feels like some weird and depressing way to have a miracle."

There was a long pause before Jill said, "Yeah, my mom is the teacher for the preschool class, so she will watch him tonight. I... uhm..." Another long pause. It felt like Jill wanted to say more but didn't know how.

After waiting for a while, Carly finally interrupted the silence. "Hey, I need to finish cleaning the dishes and go play with Joey. He's currently in the bathroom waiting for me to get him out of the bath."

"Oh, sorry. Yeah, I just wanted you to know I was praying for you and I wanted to see how you were doing. See you tonight," Jill said quickly before hanging up.

The rest of the day went by smoothly. After Joey's bath, Carly and he played games and watched one of his favorite movies. For dinner, Carly ordered a large pizza. She found herself feeling more and more nervous as the time to head out to the Bible study grew closer. She had prayed for this and wanted to go, but the way God had orchestrated events to answer her prayers made her worry.

She couldn't help the nagging thoughts. *Maybe my dad being in the hospital is my fault. Maybe God is punishing me for praying to him because I didn't say the sinner's prayer on Sunday. Maybe God is angry that I had only been thinking of myself when I prayed, and so he chose to answer my prayer by cursing my dad.*

These thoughts seemed possible, and they made her worry about what the Bible study would be like and if she would fit in.

Finally, the clock read 5:45 p.m., and Carly began packing Joey into the car to leave for church.

As Carly sat down in the driver's seat, she wanted to risk saying one more silent prayer, *God, please don't hurt anyone else in my family. I'm sorry if I caused all this mess. I just wanted to know more about you.* She buckled up and began driving.

When they got to the church, Carly was surprised by how busy it was. She had to park pretty far away from the main entrance.

As she led Joey inside the main entrance, Carly craned her neck around to look for Darcy, who told her she would help her get Joey set up for class.

"I'm at the main entrance. Where are you?" She texted.

Immediately, she heard Darcy yell her name from across the foyer.

"Oh good! Hey..." Carly was cut off from finishing as Darcy wrapped her in a big bear hug.

"Let's get Joey to his class," Darcy said as she let go of Carly.

Registering Joey into the church system was easy with Darcy's help. In no time at all, Joey was playing a game with other kids his age, and Carly was walking with Jill and Darcy to the large room on the other end of the church building where the high school students met.

"You're going to love it!" Jill said with her characteristic enthusiasm, "Pastor Dillan is so cool, and he just got married, and his wife is *so* amazing."

Carly battled against the fear raging inside her. Her stomach fluttered, her pulse was so intense she could hear her own heartbeat, and the sudden urge to run out and never come back was almost overwhelming. Jill could never understand the pain and agony she was feeling, and her excitement and cheerfulness were grating on Carly.

Just when she thought her fear would win, and she was ready to run out, Darcy grabbed her hand and gave her a squeeze. "I sit in the back a lot of the time... Where nobody can look at me," she said knowingly.

Carly gave Darcy a grateful smile and squeezed her hand back. "I think sitting in the back sounds like it's a good place for me on my first time."

Jill's eyebrows furrowed slightly. "OK, well, at least let me introduce you to Pastor Dillan before the group starts. You've had a lot of questions lately, and he is the best person I know to answer them all."

Carly couldn't explain the sudden panic she felt at having to talk to the pastor before the group started or at being forced to ask her questions to a stranger. But it was making her palms sweat, and her breathing come in rapid shallow breaths.

"Jill, let's just let God lead tonight. I think Carly should be given the chance to decide for herself if she wants to ask Pastor Dillan her questions right now. She doesn't know him like we do and she takes time to warm up to people. She is different than you." Darcy's tone was firm despite her smile.

Jill just laughed. "I know she's different, and I'm not going to force Carly to say anything." Turning to Carly, she continued, "I just want Pastor Dillan to meet you and for you to meet him. Tonight is just the beginning. There is no pressure to trust or solve anything tonight," Jill said casually.

Before Carly had time to process everything, she found that Jill had a hold of her other arm and was leading her and Darcy to the front, where the youth pastor stood talking with a couple of teenage boys who were setting up instruments and equipment.

"Hey, Pastor Dillan, this is my good friend Carly, that I told you about last week. God answered our prayers, and she was able to come today!" Jill explained cheerfully.

Carly felt her throat go dry, and her armpits started to itch as she began to sweat nervously. She hadn't realized that Jill was talking about her to this pastor behind her back. She wondered what Jill had told him.

"Hi Carly, I'm so glad you could make it. Praise God for that. Jill shared that she wanted her best friend to join us, but that you weren't able to. So, we prayed for you last week." Pastor Dillan smiled warmly as he held out his hand to shake hers.

Carly wiped her palm on her jeans before shaking his hand.

"Yeah, well, this is probably just a one-time thing. My dad is in the ICU this week, so I don't have to work. I expect my mom will make me go back to working on Wednesday nights once he is out of the hospital," Carly said flatly. She didn't know why she felt the need to manage everyone's expectations for her. But something about this whole group praying for her made her irritated.

"Oh, Carly, I'm so sorry to hear about your dad. I will be praying for a full and speedy recovery." He paused and looked intently into her eyes. "I am also praying God reassures you, and that you know this isn't punishment or a bad thing from God and that he loves your family even more than you do."

Carly's eyes immediately welled up with tears. Even though he offered her encouragement, she found she felt exposed, like everyone could see her naked, and she felt like a trapped animal. She wanted to go sit in the back and disappear. It felt like these Christians could read minds and predict the future, and it was unnerving to experience.

Her face must have been emoting some or all of this because in an instant, Darcy grabbed her hand again and said, "Thanks, Pastor Dillan. We are going to go grab a cookie before taking our seats." And just like that, Carly was trying to hold back crying while Darcy handed her a couple of chocolate chip cookies.

As Carly sat in her chair, picking at the chocolate chip cookies, she found herself wondering how these Christians just seemed to know things. *Like were there superpowers that came with being an older Christian?*

"Darcy, can Christians read minds?" she finally blurted out loud.

"What?! Of course not. Being a Christian isn't a superpower and isn't some weird magical thing. Why would you ask that?"

Carly felt dumb, but managed to mumble, "Nothing, it was just a question," before putting the whole cookie in her mouth to have an excuse not to have to speak anymore.

All around her, teenagers were talking, laughing, and seemed to be having a great time while they waited for the music to start and signal the start of the night. Carly found herself people-watching. She wanted to know how this edgy skater boy could so easily be talking to two of the most preppy-looking kids. It was as if all the rules of high school cliques didn't apply here. She even saw two kids she would have labeled Dungeons and Dragons nerds hanging out with two beefy-looking jocks. Everyone just accepted everyone else, and it didn't seem to matter how different they all looked.

"Are there ever cliques in this group?" she finally asked Darcy.

"Well, we struggle just as much as any other high school group, but Pastor Dillan said that the time before our Wednesday night starts is when you need to be practicing your "Jesus socializing skills." She used air quotes as she said this last part.

"What are Jesus socializing skills?" Carly asked with interest.

"Jesus chose the outcasts and the sinners to be his disciples and friends. He never sought out the popular or the powerful. Pastor Dillan thinks that in order for us to be more like Jesus, we need to practice seeing people like Jesus did and making friends with people we wouldn't normally be friends with."

Darcy looked around at the strange mixture of teenagers. "I guess we have been doing this practice for so long now that we are actually all friends here. See that kid over there?" she asked as she pointed to a short, acne-faced boy who was overweight and looked like he was sweating.

"That's Jeremiah. He just threw a birthday party, and his mom said that it was the first time in his entire life that everyone he invited came. She told us at the party that the last time she threw him a party, only one other kid came despite inviting over thirty kids. She said that Jesus used us to answer her prayers and that she was glad Jesus could use kids as young as us to change lives."

Darcy looked up at Carly with a misty-eyed smile. "Before Pastor Dillan's challenge about having Jesus' socializing skills, Jeremiah would never have had that many people show up. He's awkward, kinda smelly, and what he is interested in is so laser-focused on computers and computer games that most of us don't really know what he's talking about. But Jesus loves Jeremiah, so we all try to love him and see what Jesus sees. That's the challenge that we are all working on; seeing people the way Jesus does. And it's a really good feeling to know that by trying to act more like Jesus, we can actually make a difference in someone's life."

Carly nodded. She herself had benefited from her two best friends loving her when she was falling apart, and sticking with her when she was trying to push everyone away. Before she could reply to Darcy's incredible story, the music began playing loudly, and everyone began making their way to their seats. Jill was standing next to Carly with Jules and Eric to her left.

Carly looked around as teens swayed with the music, singing along no matter how badly they sang, and holding their hands high in worship. She wanted to join in with them but had so much fear holding her back.

Won't these people think I'm a fake doing what they are doing when I haven't given my life to Christ yet? I still don't really know if this religion is for me yet, anyway. My dad is in the hospital, and my family is struggling. God, please save us!

That last prayer slipped out of her thoughts, and she felt a mix of frustration and wonder that she would keep praying, even accidentally, to a God she wasn't sure liked her or loved her.

Carly did her best to sing quietly along to the worship music, but she found herself fascinated by the way these other kids her age were acting. They acted like they were at the best concert of their lives when, in reality, it was Pastor Dillan on drums, a girl singing and playing the piano, and a guy playing the guitar and singing backup. They were all good, especially the girl, but it wasn't enough to make her as excited as these other kids seemed to be. She felt like this must be one of those inexplicable Jesus things. Like they were all plugged into Jesus, and that was why they all looked electrified to be there.

After three songs, the music stopped. Pastor Dillan said a prayer over the group and then dove into his message for the night.

"Can Jesus fail you?" he asked the group. When they realized he wanted an answer, several voices shouted out, "No!"

"No?" Dillan said with a raised eyebrow. "What about when you prayed for God to help you pass that important test you forgot to study for, and then you find out you failed it? Has God failed you if he doesn't answer your prayers the way you want?"

Carly found herself leaning forward. She really wanted to know the answer to this question. Hadn't she just felt frustrated and uncertain with God because he didn't answer her prayer to attend the way she was hoping for?

The room remained quiet this time. And Pastor Dillan went on.

"What about when your aunt is sick with cancer, and you are praying for her healing? Believing every promise the Bible has about healing for her, and then God calls her home to Heaven... Has Jesus failed you then?"

At that moment, you could have heard a pen drop. The room had gone so quiet as everyone wrestled with these hard questions. Carly found herself thinking that Jesus could, in fact, fail and must not be a very powerful God if he let his believers suffer.

I want you all to open your Bibles to Psalm 34:4.

Suddenly, the room became alive again as teenagers began opening their Bibles to the spot Pastor Dillan had said. Jill reached over and helped Carly find the book of Psalms and showed her where the chapter and verse were.

Pastor Dillan read out, *"I sought the LORD, and he answered me and he delivered me from all my fears."*

"David wrote this at a time when he had been anointed as the future king of Israel, but was fleeing assassination from the current king of Israel, Saul, who was his father-in-law. He was pretending to be insane while living in a different country so that the king of that country wouldn't think of him as a threat and also try to kill him. His life was strenuous and didn't look like what he believed God had promised him his life would look like." Dillan looked into the faces of high schoolers around the room.

"Do you think God had failed David?"

A few people replied, "No!"

"No. God hadn't failed David, despite how bad his circumstances looked in that moment; God was developing David's character so that he would be a king after God's own heart. It's in Psalm 34:4 that David says that when he sought the Lord, the Lord set him free from all his fears."

"It's important to remember that God is outside of time and often chooses not to answer our prayers the way that we want or think is best because God loves us deeply and knows more than we know. It has been said that if we knew everything God knows, then we would think as God thinks. I want you to take a moment and think about the last prayer you said where you felt God didn't answer you, or at least not the way you had prayed for, and I want you to ask yourself, did God fail me?"

Carly noticed several others pull out notebooks and begin to write, so she pulled out her yellow journal and did the same.

She wrote, *"I prayed to attend Bible study, and then my dad had an accident that put him in the ICU, and my mom let me off work, and Shellie agreed to let me take Joey to church."*

Then she wrote, *"Did God fail me?"*

Well, she had made it to Bible study, so in one sense, God had answered her prayers and had given her what she asked for, but why did he have to almost kill her dad to accomplish it? It made her doubt God's reliability and goodness.

As she was thinking this, Pastor Dillan broke in, "If God doesn't answer our prayers how we want, does that mean he is untrustworthy?"

A few students said, "No."

"How many times have you prayed for something and then later on you were so glad God didn't answer that prayer the way that you had wanted? When I was your age, I prayed to marry a girl named Jackie. She was everything I thought I wanted in life, and I prayed so hard for Jackie to notice me and to want to date me."

There were a few scandalized looks around the room as Pastor Dillan's wife, Megan was sitting in the front row.

"I have never been so thankful that God didn't answer my prayers to marry Jackie. Because if he had given me what I wanted, I never would have had his best for my life and married Megan here," he said as he looked at his wife.

Several girls said, "Awe" together in unison.

"We need to remember that God is not withholding goodness. He is protecting us in ways we just don't understand. And this is a lie that humankind has been wrestling with since the very beginning. Satan has been trying to get us to believe that God is stingy and not worthy of our complete trust."

Carly looked down at her notebook and wrote, *"He is protecting us in ways we don't understand."* Anger boiled up in her.

It all felt like too much. How could God have been protecting her when her parents were trying to constantly pawn her off on each other when she was just a kid? How could God have been protecting her when she was in love with Ryan only to find out he had been using her and filming her to sell on the internet?! Where was God's protection when Kyle tried to force himself on her or when the whole school believed the lies that she knew Ryan was filming and wanted it to be all over the internet like that? Where was God's protection when every man she knew seemed to view her as a possession to own or an object to use? Why hadn't God protected her from all of the pain and sorrow and misery of the last two years?! And now, her dad was in critical condition in the hospital, and it felt like it was all her fault because she had prayed to this God to attend this Bible study. And for what!? To hear about how great this God is who allowed her to be used and abused?

She couldn't take it anymore. She grabbed her stuff, and quickly walked out of the room. She needed space to breathe.

As Carly walked out of the building to the parking lot, she noticed James. *Great, just what I need, some do-gooder to ask where I'm going.* She rolled her eyes and hoped he wouldn't say anything.

"Carly!" came James' voice. "Are you guys done already?" he asked as he walked toward her.

Carly didn't stop for him and curtly replied, "No," as she walked out of the front entrance.

Just as she was about to sit on the bench in front of the building, James caught up with her.

"Hey, what's wrong? Is everything OK?" he asked as he looked at her face. Carly was breathing hard and trying to hold back sobs, and this awkward dude was so infuriating. Couldn't he see that she wanted to be alone?

She couldn't hold back all of the pain inside any longer, and she let loose on James.

"No, James, everything is not OK!" she practically yelled. "You all want me to buy into some story of a loving and caring God who saves people from their miserable lives and is all-knowing and all-good, but look around the world for five minutes, and you'll see that this just isn't true! God put my dad in the ICU because I prayed to come to this stupid Bible study! If my dad dies, I will never follow this God. I swear it!" she screamed through her tears and frustration.

James' face showed concern. He grabbed Carly's shoulders and gently led her to sit on the bench.

"Carly, let's sit down and talk about this. You bring up some really good points that people have been trying to work out for a lot longer than we've been alive." His voice was so calm and gentle that Carly just stared at him.

How could he be so calm when I just accused him of believing in a fake god? she thought to herself while they took a seat on the bench.

"You bring up an age-old question. If God is all-powerful and all-good, why does he allow sin, pain, and suffering to exist?" James said as he scooted just a little further away from her.

Carly couldn't remember ever asking anything, but she did want to know the answer to that question.

"I think people who have experienced pain and suffering all come to this question at some point; I know that this one really plagued me a few years ago when my brother died."

Carly felt alarmed. She had no idea that James had ever gone through anything hard. All of these Christians just seemed like happy, oblivious do-gooders who didn't know the first thing about the real world or pain.

"I'm sorry," she whispered.

As James locked eyes with her, Carly couldn't help but notice that they were a gorgeous shade of blue.

He hesitated for a moment before saying, "I was in charge of watching my siblings, but Jack was always so difficult. He never listened to me, and I was always so hard on him."

James looked down, trying to find the words to share something he would rather not talk about, or so it looked to Carly.

She was just about to tell him he didn't have to tell her anything else when James seemed to find the courage to go on.

"He had snuck off to his friend's house without my knowing. He was supposed to be up in his room doing homework, but his friend, who had just gotten his license, came and picked him up while I was playing video games." James swallowed hard like he had just admitted to a terrible crime.

"When I realized he was gone, I was in a rage. He was only fifteen and was not allowed to just leave the house without telling anyone where he was. I called my parents, and they were understandably angry at both of us. My mom told me to call his best friend Matt to see if they had gone for a joy ride since she knew he had just gotten his license. I called Matt's house, and sure enough, Jack was there. I was so angry. By the time I arrived to pick him up, I was shouting at how irresponsible and selfish he was. The entire drive home, I was determined to make him regret his decision by telling him how wrong he was, and trying to make him feel small. I was so focused on berating him that I never saw the light turn red. I was already speeding because I was so angry, and when I drove into the intersection, a Ford F150 plowed straight into my passenger side. They say that Jack died instantly." James looked up into Carly's eyes, his filled with tears.

His voice shook as he continued. "My last words to my brother were unkind, cruel, and filled with hate. And worse than all of that, his death is my fault. I ran that stupid red light. I let my anger get the best of me. I killed my own brother."

He broke down crying for a moment before he could regain control of his voice. "I have wondered every day for the past two years why God allowed Jack to die. Why did God allow my brother to suffer from my stupid choices? Why did God allow me to become a murderer?"

James became so emotional he stood up and turned his back to Carly. Carly felt compassion flood her heart as she watched James' remorse for one moment of unchecked anger plague him with guilt.

"James," Carly said as she stood up and walked toward him. "I don't really know much about God, but I do know a lot about bad people. You're not a bad guy, James. I know you probably hate yourself for what happened to your brother, but that is actually proof that you aren't a bad guy. Bad guys are never sorry over all the people they hurt."

"Carly," he said as he kept his back to her, "I murdered my brother in my heart long before I ever ran the red light that caused his death. Sin is a heart issue that comes to life in deed and action. When Adam and

Eve sinned in the garden, they cursed all humanity with sinful lives. Christ is the only hope of rescue from living life as an eternal villain." He turned to face her and was visibly surprised that she was only a foot away.

Carly placed her hand on his arm to offer comfort and reassurance. "I'm so sorry for your loss, James. Thank you for sharing your story with me. I have been feeling like an outsider. Like I'm some angry, unhappy monster desperately trying to convince all these cheerful people I'm one of them and feeling like a total fraud. Your story was a good reminder that you really never know what someone has gone through, and that I shouldn't judge people based on my own assumptions." Carly squeezed his arm before letting go.

James looked into her eyes and said, "Carly, humans have been making terrible choices from the very beginning because God gave us the gift of free will. He wanted us to choose to walk in a loving and intimate relationship with him, but we chose our own selfish path instead. Humankind has been suffering from trying to elevate ourselves to the same level as God ever since. That is why God sent his own son to die a humiliating death for our sins. If there had been any other way, it wouldn't have taken the suffering and death of Jesus to give us a chance at a new life, a life in a relationship with the triune God."

James' eyes were still filled with tears when he said, "I had thought that I was a pretty good person who never did anything wrong before I became a murderer. But now I understand my desperate need for Jesus and how empty and pathetic all my works were to be good enough on my own. I think some of us are slow learners, and it takes God giving us the consequences of our sins to show us just how deep and wide the chasm is between us and Him. Without Jesus, there is no way to breach the distance and come close to God. I think God allows sin so that we understand who we actually are before him and why we desperately need him."

Carly wasn't sure what to make of that. It felt a lot like manipulation to her, and she still didn't feel like God was trustworthy. But she didn't want to hurt or upset James any more than he had already been. So, she just said, "Thanks for sharing."

Carly looked at her watch and realized that it was already 8 p.m. People were congregating in the foyer, and she needed to get her brother home for bedtime.

"I have to go pick up my brother and get him home for bedtime. It's pretty late for that little dude. His mom normally has him in bed by now." Carly waved goodbye as she walked back into the church.

On the drive home, Carly kept wrestling with the thoughts in her mind, *How could an all-wise, all-powerful, and all-loving God allow people to suffer like she had, like her dad, like James, and his family? Why would a good God allow suffering?*

James' words and these thoughts swirled in her mind and made her question every experience she had had over the past week. Like her being given a journal and Bible the first day she stepped foot into a church or the overwhelming peace and joy she felt after she had tried praying. She couldn't deny that she had been happier, lighter, and less cynical these past few days, but at the same time, there were too many questions she had. Like why did God smite her dad when she had prayed to go to Bible study? Why hadn't he simply had her mom hire a new employee? It seemed to her that God was like a strong and powerful force, but that he couldn't be sentient or all-wise since he didn't seem to know how to answer prayers properly. But this thought didn't match up with what the pastors at Darcy's church had taught.

She just wished she knew what to believe.

And then, as if someone else had whispered in her ear, she heard the words, *Why not pray about it?*

Just as Carly was about to whisper a short prayer, Joey yawned and whimpered, "I want my mommy!"

"I know, buddy. We're almost home, and your mommy should be home to tuck you into bed," Carly soothed.

But Joey had had enough and cried the rest of the way home.

Chapter 15: Meeting God

T he next morning, Carly woke with the same heavy wrestling spirit that had bothered her the night before. When she had gotten home last night, it was a scramble to get Joey into bed and catch Shellie up on the day's events. Then she and Shellie had stayed up for a while talking about her dad, about the miscarriage, and trying to figure out how to get through this uncertain time.

So much had taken place and been talked about that Carly realized she hadn't prayed once after Bible study. The thought seemed strange. Until the past week, she had never prayed, and now feeling irritated that she had forgotten to pray when she had wanted to seemed laughable.

The clock on her phone read 6:57 a.m. Carly had wanted to sleep in since she was exempt from school for the rest of this week, but it seemed her body was in autopilot mode. As she was about to start playing a game on her phone, she noticed her Bible and journal sitting beside her on the coffee table.

Carly set down her phone, picked up her Bible, and decided to do a little experiment. She prayed, "God, please tell me if you are wise."

Carly held her Bible with the spine facing her makeshift bed on the couch and gently let her hands fall, allowing the book to open to a random page.

It fell open, and her eyes read Romans 11:33.

"Oh, the depth of the riches and wisdom and knowledge of God! How unsearchable are his judgments and how inscrutable his ways!"

Carly gasped, and her arms became covered with goosebumps. This was too strange! Suddenly, she felt as though her Bible was possessed by some spirit as if it were some sort of Ouija board. Carly sat motionless for a moment, trying to decide if this was just some strange coincidence or if the God of the Bible was actually trying to communicate with her.

Abruptly, she shot out of her makeshift bed, and her Bible dropped to the floor as she took several steps away from it. Carly didn't feel fear exactly, but she had just prayed a question about God's wisdom, and then her Bible seemed to answer her with that verse about how God is wise and just. It was intense enough to make her want to run away, but somehow, she felt a deep pull in her spirit. She needed to know what else this book said about God. Carly looked at the page. At the top corner, it read "Romans." She didn't know what that meant, but she decided to flip to the front of the Book of Romans and just start reading this section.

The first seven verses of the first chapter were a confusing jumble of words and salutations that Carly couldn't make much out of. Then it went on, and this author, Paul, said that everyone should know God just by looking at the sky and earth. This felt too harsh to Carly. She was almost eighteen and had never once stopped to look at the sky and earth and thought, *I should be worshiping Jesus.*

Carly went to the window and peered out at the sky. She looked at the beautiful puffy clouds floating by, and for the first time in her life, she wondered, *How do tons of water float effortlessly in the air? Who makes all this happen in harmony?* She looked out into the front yard and saw Shellie's flower bed filled with brightly colored flowers and a couple of yellow butterflies flitting around in it. She noticed a bee buzzing from flower to flower.

For the first time in her life, she thought, *it can't be by accident that all of this is here. These plants and insects working in perfect harmony together can't be the result of a big bang. These were carefully and lovingly designed to work in harmony with each other.*

Carly felt an overwhelming urge to be a butterfly delicately flying by the flowers. She felt that to live according to your purpose, must bring harmony and joy.

She looked back at the couch, where her blankets and Bible were still on the floor, and decided she would try this strange power out again.

Carly sat back down and whispered, "What is my purpose? How can I be happy like the butterfly?"

She held out her Bible, then let her hands drop down quickly so the covers flopped back, opening the Bible to a random spot. Not knowing if this would work a second time, Carly desperately hoped it would.

Her Bible opened to a different spot this time, and as she looked down at the page. She read Ecclesiastes 12:13. *"The end of the matter; all has been heard. Fear God and keep his commandments, for this is the whole duty of man."*

Fear God? Carly wondered to herself. *How can my purpose be to fear God? I thought Jesus was supposed to be approachable and all that.*

Carly felt her heart sink. She felt as though her Bible's magic must have ended because that didn't seem like an answer. She tossed her Bible across her makeshift bed, and as it hit the other arm of the couch, it flopped open yet again. Carly sat there staring at it irritably. She had wanted to know how to be happy and how to have the good life which the pastor said Jesus died to give her. She wanted to know why pain and suffering were everywhere, even in the church where people had dedicated their entire lives to following him. *What is the point of following a God who didn't spare his people pain and misery and didn't even spare his own son?* She thought in outrage.

She reached over and grabbed her Bible. It was opened to James 1. As her eyes landed on the second verse, it was like she was being sucked into the page as she read through the verses.

She read, *"Count it all joy, my brothers, when you meet trials of various kinds, for you know that the testing of your faith produces steadfastness. And let steadfastness have its full effect, that you may be perfect and complete, lacking in nothing."*

Something clicked in Carly, and even though she knew she shouldn't understand this strange and backward passage, she felt herself thinking the phrase, *What doesn't kill you makes you stronger.*

She looked at the few verses again and read them slowly. She found herself wishing she was perfect and complete and needed nothing and no one. This book promised that she would eventually be perfect and complete if she endured troubles of any kind. Carly craved completion. She felt as though she had known too much trouble in her short life and the idea that God could somehow use it to make her better evoked a deep yearning in her.

Like a gentle whisper in her mind, Carly heard, *Everyone suffers, but I redeem the suffering of those who are my children. Give your life to me and live redeemed.*

And then suddenly, understanding flooded her. God had created a perfect world where there was both perfect justice and intimate love. But when Adam and Eve broke the one law he gave them, his justice could not go unfulfilled, and they were sentenced to a broken, sin-filled life. The Earth and all of humanity were cursed to live a life full of the consequences of sin. Somehow, without being able to explain it, Carly knew that God, the Father, sacrificed his own son, Jesus, to take on what should have been her punishment so that she could escape hell and separation from God, the source of goodness, and instead walk in his love. Carly knew that the reason she had felt peace in her life over the past week was because God had been with her, restoring her, and filling her. Even though nothing in her life had improved or changed for the better, she still felt peace and lightness in her soul. Somehow, Carly knew this peace came from God: from believing that Jesus understood her and loved her.

Carly's hands were still on her Bible as she sat cuddled in blankets on the couch when she heard, B*e holy as I am holy.* Carly didn't have the first idea of what this meant, and it felt strange to think of something she couldn't understand.

But suddenly, she heard this sort of voice tell her so clearly, *I want you to take delight in my presence so that you can spread that delight to others who are filled with misery like you were.*

Carly wept. She suddenly understood that Christ's suffering was nothing like her own. He suffered so that he could rescue her; she suffered because she was a slave to sin. He died because he loved her and so that she could be set free, and all that he asked of her was to love him with her whole heart. Carly had never known a man she could trust with her whole heart. She had been seen as a nuisance and then a free servant by her dad, an object for pleasure by her boyfriend and other guys, and then worthless by men she wouldn't debase herself for. Yet Jesus had worked so many strange happenings to tell her that he loved her so much he died to rescue her from the misery that was her life.

Still weeping, Carly wanted so badly to know what to say or do to tell Jesus that she loved him and wanted to surrender to his love for her. She vaguely remembered what the pastor had said on Sunday, and so she did her best to pray and tell God that she was committing to his way of life.

Carly prayed, "Father God, thank you for sending Jesus to suffer a horrible life so that mine could be redeemed. I have lived a sinful life before I knew about you. I made a lot of bad choices trying to find satisfaction and meaning in this world. Please forgive me for getting it wrong. Wash me clean from my past, and let me live a new life with you. Help me let go of the wrong that was done to me and the wrong I have done. I don't want to be the broken girl that I have been: always angry, always afraid, always miserable, and paranoid that men are out to get me and use and abuse me. I want to be set free. Amen"

Her prayer wasn't anything like the prayer that the pastor had led the others in, but it was her way of telling God she wanted the redeemed life he offered and that she was ready to live a new way.

As Carly wiped her eyes with her blankets and set her Bible back on the coffee table, Shellie walked into the living room and told her, "Your dad just woke up and is being moved out of the ICU! Get dressed. We're all going to go see him as soon as we're ready." Just as abruptly as she came into the living room, Shellie was off, running to Joey's room to get him ready, too.

Carly dressed quickly. She had time to make coffee and toast while she waited for Shellie and Joey to finish getting ready. Her heart felt so light, and she was filled with so much radiant joy that she could barely sit still and stop grinning.

Chapter 16: Hospital Healing

The drive to the hospital was short. Carly spent the entire journey praying for her dad, that he would be all there mentally and that he wouldn't be in pain. Carly wondered if he would know or remember anything about what she had last said to him on the night when she first saw him. She worried that her dad would want nothing to do with her and the closer they got to the hospital the more nervous she felt. But Carly was used to feeling unwanted and had years of practice looking outwardly calm.

When they got to the floor where her dad's new room was, Carly's stomach was churning. Suddenly she felt as if the coffee and toast she had scarfed down were a terrible mistake. She looked at Joey and he seemed to look a little scared too. Shellie was holding his hand and Carly took his other hand. In that moment all of the anxiety, pain, and fear she had been bottling up began to explode and it took everything in Carly to not fall over. Her breath began to quicken as she walked slowly with Joey and Shellie.

"Carly, why is your hand wet?" Joey said in disgust as he pulled his little hand out of hers. Carly's hands were sweating from the anxiety coursing through her. Shellie looked at her in alarm.

"Carly, you don't have to go in and see him if it is too much for you. You and Joey…"

"No!" Carly snapped louder than she had meant. It was like she had lost control of her body and it was doing weird things. She cleared her throat to try again.

"No, Shellie. I want to see my dad. I am just afraid he isn't going to want to see me, that he never wants me, and it's hard to walk in and face that kind of rejection."

Shellie's eyes were full of sadness and pity for what Carly had just told her. She gave Carly a quick hug and said, "Your dad loves you, he's just too stubborn and foolish to show it most of the time."

Carly felt stunned. She had never heard Shellie ever criticize her dad before, but this was the kindest and most encouraging thing she could have said in that moment.

"I hope you're right," Carly said as she looked into Shellie's eyes.

Together, Shellie, Carly, and Joey walked into room 207 and found Nick laughing with an elderly nurse who looked too much like no-nonsense to be laughing with him. But there they were enjoying some joke together.

Joey was the first to break the barrier. "Daddy!" he yelled as he ran up to Nick's bedside.

Shellie had packed Joey a bag full of books and dinosaurs and cars and now he was hurriedly trying to show all of them to Nick.

Nick looked like he was being made comfortable, but still couldn't move much. His arm and foot were both in casts and the blankets were up to his neck. Shellie ran quickly over to Joey to get him to move all his toys off the bed and over to the two chairs in the corner of the room.

Just then, Nick looked up and saw Carly. "Carly!" he said in a choked voice. "I was hoping you would be here." He motioned her closer, and Carly's legs obeyed before she had time to even think about what she was doing. As soon as Carly stood close enough to Nick, he reached out with his good hand as if asking her to hold his hand. She took it.

"Carly, I need to tell you something. But I don't want to alarm Joey. Hey Shell, can you put on the TV for me? Put on some cartoons please."

Carly couldn't remember the last time her dad asked Shellie to do anything nicely. Normally, he just sauntered in, gave commands with a smile and wink, and expected no one would dare defy such charming orders. But he actually said please this time, her dad was acting differently than the man she had known him to be just a few short days earlier.

"Carly, I want you to know that I heard every word. I can't really explain how, but it was like I was having an out-of-body experience. Like I wasn't sure I wanted to go back into my body. And then your words pierced me. You asked me to stay with you even though your whole life I had been in a constant state of abandoning you." Nick wiped a few tears from his eyes and then returned his good hand to Carly's.

"You can't imagine how your words impacted me in that moment. It was like all of a sudden, I had hope that maybe I hadn't ruined every good thing in my life with my own relentless, compelling selfishness. I wanted so badly to come back to my body so that I could hold your hand and tell you what I was never brave enough to say before. I love you Carly girl. When you were born, I felt how unprepared and inadequate I was to be your father and instead of trying to man up and grow into the dad you needed, I ran away believing that your life would be better if you didn't have me ruining it. I had ruined so many important things in my life and I didn't want to ruin you too. I didn't leave you or your mom because of you." He gave Carly's hand a squeeze.

"I left because of me. I was scared and selfish. I left because I thought it was the best thing I could do for you because I was confused. I'm sorry Mija. I never meant to hurt you like that." Nicked pulled his hand out of Carly's to wipe more tears and he began to cry harder. Just then, several monitors began to beep and his smiling older nurse came back in looking more like the no-nonsense version of herself.

She checked the monitor pads on his chest and all the connecting wires. "It looks like you're overdoing it," she said as she placed the finger monitor back on his casted arm. "Your blood oxygen levels are still struggling and I need you to take a break."

She gave a stern glance at Carly, Shellie, and Joey. "He is out of critical condition, but that doesn't mean he is back to his normal self. His lungs are recovering nicely, but are still weakened which means he shouldn't be doing anything strenuous." She looked pointedly at Carly as if to say, *"Stop making him cry and talk."* Carly understood the hint.

"Do we have to leave the room?" Carly asked timidly.

"No," Nick said firmly. "I am allowed visitors and I want you all here with me."

Carly looked into her dad's eyes and saw something she couldn't remember ever seeing before. It was like his eyes suddenly had a fire behind them and he seemed more alive than she had ever remembered him being.

When the nurse left, Carly's dad stretched out his good hand to her once again. Carly walked back over to him and took hold of her dad's hand. It was strange to be holding his hand now that she was almost fully grown. Her whole life she had wanted to be able to hold her dad's hand and feel safe and loved, but it wasn't until this very moment, looking into the bruised hues in her dad's face that she felt loved by him.

"Carly, I'm sorry for hurting you. For making you feel abandoned and unwanted. I have always been so proud of you and I'm just sorry it's taken me almost eighteen years to tell you this," Nick said as he squeezed her hand.

Carly felt hot tears slip down her cheeks. This was a broken place in her soul and her dad's confession was like a doctor trying to reset a bone. It hurt in the moment, but she knew she would be better off for having it done.

"Dad, thank you for everything you've said. It helps. But I have to know, why did you stay for Joey, when you never stayed for me? I always felt like if I had been born a son, you would have stayed." Carly was crying and she struggled with feeling like she was going directly against the stern nurse's warning, but she had to know and this was the only time her dad and she had ever had an honest conversation.

"Mija, by the time I met Shellie, I was ready to end my own pathetic life. I had blown through women like they were cheap cigarettes and nothing I had done had ever made me feel any better. Everything I was doing made me feel worse. When I met Shellie, I had hit rock bottom. But Shellie loved me as I was while still expecting me to grow up. She pushed me to be a better man than I ever thought possible, but she didn't ever make me feel small. She just inspired me to be bigger. I don't know how to explain it, but she's good for me. With your mom, I always felt intimidated by her dreams and ambitions. I wanted to be the big provider, but she had really high expectations that I couldn't ever measure up to and it made me feel three inches tall. It's not her fault, it's just how I felt. With Shellie, she looked at me like I had already won all the prizes, Like I was somebody special, and when I told her I had done nothing, she would just tell me 'Not yet, maybe but you could.' By the time Joey came into the picture I knew I wanted a second chance to get it right, to learn from the mistakes I had made with you and your mom. I wanted to be the better man Shellie believed I could be. It was never about loving them more; it was that I just didn't know how to be that same man around you when you looked so hurt and angry with me. I'm sorry."

Those last words, Nick barely whispered as his lower lip began to tremble in with the weight of eighteen years of suppressed emotions.

Carly felt her own heart stir. Her mom was tough to be around. She was the perfect perfectionist and she expected perfection and strength from everyone around her. Carly had often felt herself crumbling under the weight of trying to live up to her mom's high standards. It was enough to drive anyone who could leave away. Her mom Heidi was smart, talented, driven, hardworking, and fiercely determined. She was not a bad mother or person, but she was critical. Carly had grown up under her critical eye and she knew first-hand how suffocating it could be.

She knew she didn't want to be a critical perfectionist, but she had spent a lifetime learning that voice in her head telling her to be and do better. In this moment, she just wanted to know how to process and what to say. She thought her prayer, *Oh God help me. I want a good relationship with my dad, one filled with love and understanding. Please help me know what to do or say.*

Carly looked at her dad and then it just flowed, "Dad, when you left mom, she always blamed you and me. She blamed your weakness, and she blamed me for driving you away. When I went to live with you after Joey was born, I thought maybe we could be a family, but you treated me so coldly. You were so different with me than how you treated Shellie and Joey. I felt like you only wanted me with you, so you could have a free babysitter. After things went wrong with Ryan, I tried reaching out to you, but you took Ryan's side even though he broke my heart. It felt like you would rather have him as your kid than me. So, I left to go live with Mom." Carly was crying. Her tears flowed freely.

Just then Shellie spoke up, "Joey and I are going to grab some food from the cafeteria for lunch. We will get enough for everyone and bring it back in here." She kissed Nick's forehead and then they walked out.

"Carly, I never meant to take Ryan's side. I just wanted you to not be so broken up about that guy. You were too young to be so broken hearted over some guy. I'm sorry, Mija. I didn't mean to drive you away." Nick was crying again.

Carly was scared that if her dad was too upset, she would actually cause him physical pain. She squeezed his hand. "I love you Dad. I always have and I always will. Thank you for everything you said and for fighting to stay alive. We can talk more about this when you get out of here." She leaned over and for the first time in many years, she kissed her dad's cheek.

Carly pulled a chair closer to his bed and they sat watching cartoons holding hands for another twenty minutes before Shellie and Joey came in with sandwiches, fruit cups, and a few cookies.

The rest of the morning was spent chatting as one big happy family. Carly couldn't believe it. If someone had told her just a couple days ago that she would feel like she belonged to her father and step-mom, like they loved her just as much as their own son, she would have laughed and ridiculed them for having such a stupid idea. Now, this felt so good, like it was always meant to be like this. Joey was crashing dinosaurs into Hot Wheels cars making all manner of strange sounds, while Shellie and Nick talked about when Nick would get out of the hospital and how they would try to grow their family again. Carly made them both laugh with terrible baby name suggestions and occasionally threw cars at the dinosaurs to make Joey laugh too.

As she sat in her chair nibbling a cookie, Carly felt in her heart that God was using all these things in her life for good somehow.

Chapter 17
Senior Skip Day

Friday morning, Carly was still at Shellie and Nick's house. She was just starting to get out of her cozy couch bed when her phone buzzed. She answered it with a quiet, "Hello?"

"Carly!" She heard Darcy and Jill scream from the other end. She had to pull her phone away from her ear they were so loud.

"We are going to the beach. Want to come?" Darcy shouted.

"Sorry Darc, I didn't pack a swimsuit and I think I am going to the hospital to go be with my dad now that he's out of his coma," Carly said quietly, but she hoped firmly.

Suddenly there was honking outside of her house that echoed in the phone.

Carly felt her stomach drop. She could tell by the way Darcy was giggling on the phone they were already in her driveway.

"How did you know where I would be?" she asked over the phone.

"I stopped by your house first and your mom told us. She even let us come in and grab your swimsuit and a towel for you," Darcy shouted back.

As Carly opened the door to see her two friends in Jill's car, she saw her swimsuit being dangled out of the passenger window in Darcy's hand.

Carly hung up as she walked over to Darcy.

She smiled despite herself at how bubbly and excited her two friends were. She had wanted to be part of the senior skip day plans more than anything, but things were different now. Her dad was awake and they had things to talk about.

She grabbed her bikini out of Darcy's hand. "I wish I could go; it looks like it's going to be the perfect weather for a fun beach day, but my dad is awake and I need to be there for him."

Jill and Darcy exchanged a disappointed look before Jill replied, "We knew it was a long shot. We just felt like you've missed so many things last year and we wanted to make sure you got to really enjoy all the perks of being a senior this year."

Just then Shellie walked out with Joey right behind her, still in his jammies.

"What's all this?" Shellie asked in bemusement.

"Darcy and Jill want me to go to the beach with them for senior skip day," Carly replied flatly.

"Awe, that sounds so fun. You should go," Shellie said as she winked at Darcy and Jill.

"We made plans to go to the hospital and spend the day with Dad. I don't want to miss that," Carly replied with some emotion.

Shellie took Carly by the shoulder and pulled her a little away from Jill's car which was still blaring pop music loudly.

Facing Carly, Shellie said, "I know yesterday your dad and you had a great conversation that was long overdue, but his newfound openness about his love for you isn't going to go away because you choose to have fun today and do something for yourself. I promise you that your dad has wanted to find a way to be able to say these things to you for a while now. Go to the beach and enjoy your senior skip day with your friends. We are not going anywhere and your dad will understand. I promise."

Shellie looked intently into Carly's eyes as she spoke. It was as if she was hoping the intensity of her stare would impart how deeply she meant each word.

"I've waited my whole life to hear him say he loves me and is proud of me. I don't want to waste today going to the beach when we could continue our conversation," Carly said as a tear rolled down her cheek.

"Carly, sweetheart, experiencing a fun beach day with your best friends is not a waste. And honestly, Nurse-No-Nonsense would probably kick us out if we make your dad cry again today. Let's be patient for that conversation. You can see him tomorrow morning and tell him all about your day today. I think your mom will also have a fit if you don't go. She has already called me twice and sent me this text message."

Shellie pulled up the message and showed it to Carly. It read, "*You had better let her go to the beach. She deserves a fun day after how hard this week has been for her and how much she has slaved away for you!*"

Carly cringed at the ungracious accusations in her mom's text that mirrored what she herself had said to Heidi not two days ago.

"OK. I guess you're right," Carly relented.

Wiping her tears away, she turned around and gave an unenthusiastic "woot-woot" to her friends who were making silly dance moves and goofy faces at Joey to try and get him to laugh. Joey was thoroughly enjoying the silliness and fun.

"Can I go too!" He half-yelled, half-begged.

"No love, you are going to go eat your breakfast and then you and I are going to go get a new toy to take and share with Daddy."

"Yaaayyy!" Joey yelled as Shellie ushered him back inside.

Carly looked at her friends and then at herself. "Um, I need to get beach ready before I can go. She said as she rubbed her prickly legs. It's been a crazy week and I wasn't planning on this."

Darcy laughed. "We figured as much," she said as she handed Carly a bag with all her things from her shower at her mom's house.

"We thought you might want this too." She grinned.

Carly stood stunned at how well Darcy knew her and had thought through all of the reasons she might say no.

Jill leaned over and turned the music down. "We are going to drive to Starbucks and grab us some coffee and breakfast. We will bring yours back to you. That should give you about twenty minutes to get ready before we are back again. Does that work?"

"Yeah, that should be enough time. I take it you two brought sunscreen and made lunch plans? Or should I make a sandwich while I'm getting ready?" Carly asked.

"Nope! We are meeting Jules and James for lunch at the Carl's Jr. next to the beach and then they are going to help us set up for a bonfire. A bunch of people are coming and my mom and dad will bring us hotdogs and all the things to eat for dinner," Jill said excitedly.

"Wow! That all sounds amazing," Carly said cheerfully, but her stomach fluttered at the thought of getting to hang out with James again. As Carly went back inside, she told herself to stop being ridiculous. *A guy like James would never think twice about a girl like me. He is way too good for someone like me and I'm sure he knows it.* Yet every time she thought about him her stomach did that little flutter and her heart skipped a beat and she scolded herself for being so ridiculous.

By the time Jill and Darcy pulled up with Carly's Caramel Macchiato and breakfast sandwich, and the girls were on their way to the beach it was 10 a.m. Their drive to the beach was loud with

Jill's Christian pop music and the sound of the wind as they drove down the coast with their hands out the windows. When they parked, Carly noticed a few other clusters of teenagers near them, all probably skipping school for the same reason. Her heart sank in fear that she might run into people from school, or worse, Kyle.

She began looking at the other clusters of teenagers more closely.

"Hey," Darcy said, coming up and putting one arm around her shoulders. "It's going to be a fun day. We have prayed that it would be good, safe, and fun. You don't need to look so worried."

"I just thought that other seniors from school might also have the same idea as us," Carly said meaningfully.

"Oh," was all Darcy said as concern flickered across her face and she began taking a closer look at the groups across the beach.

Jill walked up with arms loaded down with blankets and chairs. She dropped everything as she noticed the worried looks on Carly and Darcy's faces as they looked intently at everyone else they could see at the beach.

"What are we doing?" Jill asked as she stood next to them.

"Carly's worried that certain losers from school or their older friend might be here too," Darcy said meaningfully.

"Oh," was Jill's reply.

After standing and staring in silence for a minute longer, Jill was the first to break the silence. "It kinda feels like this day is already under attack. I think we need to pray together. Let's hold hands and pray really quick. Come on, give me your hands," she said bossily as she held out her hands expectantly.

Darcy and Carly obeyed and grabbed her hands and Jill immediately closed her eyes and began.

"Father, thank you for this glorious sunshiny day and the warm weather and cool breezes. We ask that you put a hedge of protection around us today. That no enemy would be able to torture our bodies, minds, or spirits. We pray against demonic attacks and we pray against bullies and people who would seek to harm and offend us. We ask that you shield us from all unwanted attention and that we would be able to enjoy this carefree day at the beach. In Jesus' precious name, we pray, Amen."

"Amen," Carly and Darcy mumbled after her.

Carly looked around and couldn't find a single familiar face. "I'm just being paranoid I guess," she finally said to her friends, as she offered a sheepish smile.

"It was a good reminder that we needed more prayer," Jill said in her typical optimistic fashion. "Oh! I forgot. And God please don't let us get sunburns or jellyfish and stingray stings. Amen" She smiled brightly. "That is my usual beach prayer," she said with a laugh.

The girls loaded up their arms and made a camp near the bonfire pit and one close to the water's edge.

Only two hours before they would put their swim covers and flip-flops back on and walk to Carl's Jr. to meet up with Jules and James.

"Is anyone else coming to lunch or is it just Jules and James?" Carly tried to ask nonchalantly.

Darcy raised an eyebrow up at her. "Why? Anyone special you wish was coming?" she asked suspiciously.

Carly laughed, "Nope. I just thought maybe Josh and Eric would make an appearance today," Carly said trying to deflect attention off herself.

Darcy just grinned. "Oh, they are coming to the bonfire. Eric made plans to go to the mountains and see if they could snowboard. He and a few guys from church left last night and plan on driving back in time for dinner. And Josh said he and his buddies were going skydiving today. They both sound insane if you ask me but that's boys for you." She laughed as she flopped onto her stomach to let her back tan.

"I'm glad they are coming," Carly said with a laugh as she also rolled onto her stomach.

"And what about you? Any special someone you would like to invite? Maybe Daniel?" Darcy said with a playful wink.

Carly looked flatly back at her. "Things with Daniel didn't work out. Turns out Jessica was right. We were too different. And honestly, he was so handsome and such a smooth talker it made me nervous. Like literally, everywhere we went some girl was flirting with him. Plus, when I was busy trying to press charges against Kyle, Daniel got bored and ended things, so there's that too."

Carly tried to keep her tone casual and light. She didn't want Darcy to know how hurt she felt about the abrupt way things had ended with Daniel or that she was catching feelings for James despite herself.

"Oh girl, I didn't know. I mean, I know things ended, but you never really talked about it at the time. What happened?"

"We went on a couple of dates, and I felt a lot of red flags going off, but told myself I was just being crazy because of my past. He called me several times to try and go out again, but I didn't answer or call back because I was too worked up about dealing with my past and things just fizzled. By the time I finally texted him back, he made it clear he had moved on and wished me the best. End of story. It was a little fling that gave me hope that I might one day have a normal relationship and I will cherish that little flame of hope, but Daniel wasn't right for me. Jessica was right, we were just too different."

Darcy pulled her sunglasses down to look at Carly more intently. "Girl, I'm glad you've moved on because between you and me I think James has a thing for you."

"What!?" Carly shouted and felt her face going red. "What makes you think that?" she asked more composedly.

"Well, he was supposed to go snowboarding with Eric and the other guys, but when he found out that Jules was going to meet up with us for lunch, he changed his plans and decided to come too. We even told him you might not even come, but he said he would rather have lunch with the ladies than get beat up on a snowboard with the guys." Darcy laughed.

"Well, that doesn't mean he likes me, Darc. That just means he liked our lunch plans better than snowboarding. And honestly, who could blame him?" Carly said, trying to get her stomach under control since the butterflies had taken over again.

"Well, he didn't like our lunch plans until your name got brought up, so if you ask me, he has a thing for you," Darcy replied as she pushed her sunglasses back up and sniffed haughtily.

Carly just laughed. It felt like a thousand years had passed since she had had a normal, silly conversation about the boys they liked or who liked them with Darcy and it felt good to be doing something normal.

Jill, who had been putting up the umbrella next to the bonfire pit they were saving, had walked back to their spot closer to the water. "Girls, I'm sweating. Let's go boogie boarding for a bit and then we can dry off before we have to walk to Carl's Jr for lunch."

Carly was starting to feel sweaty too. She and Darcy stood up, grabbed their boards, and headed into the water. The water was cool and refreshing. It cleared Carly's mind and somehow made her feel at peace with the world. This day had not turned out the way that she had planned. She had wanted to talk more with her dad, she had wanted to hear that he still loved her and cared about her, but somehow, today not going to plan felt like a gift. She got to live this carefree day with her best friends before she was to graduate and take on all the cares of the world. As Carly floated on her borrowed boogie board and laughed with Jill and Darcy, she felt a sort of twinge inside of her. Like something in her spirit had realigned. Somehow, suddenly she could see the world differently. She couldn't explain why, but she just knew that there were seasons of pain and suffering, but that they didn't last forever. She also felt certain that now that she had Jesus in her heart, she could get through those future hard seasons until she was able to find days like this one; where the sky was blue, the sun was warm, and her heart was full of laughter.

Carly caught a wave and rode it into the beach. Just as she was getting out of the water, she noticed that Jill had also caught the same wave. "That was a good one huh?" she shouted to Jill over the sound of crashing waves.

"Yeah, it was!" Jill shouted back as she looked at the watch on her wrist. "Hey, I think we had better get dried off and start walking over. It's a little past 11:30 a.m. and it will take us at least fifteen minutes to walk over," Jill said as she started waving for Darcy to come in.

Darcy caught the next wave and rode that into the shore. "Is it time?" she asked knowingly.

"Yup, let's dry off and head over," Jill replied.

"Good, I'm starving already," Darcy said grinning.

Carly just laughed. She couldn't remember the last time she had felt this light and carefree. Before, when she had a good day, she would have wasted the whole day looking for things to go wrong, for the other shoe to drop. She would have been so preoccupied with her own grief, pain, and anger that she could never allowed herself to just enjoy the few good days that she did have to enjoy. But today, the sound of her own genuine laughter reminded her that Jesus was in her heart making her into something new.

As the girls put on their clothes over their swimsuits and grabbed their bags with their valuables that they had hidden under their towels, Carly began to feel her pulse race and her stomach flutter. *Ugh, you have got to stop this. He's just a guy!* she scolded herself.

When they got to the Carl's Jr. a few moments later, Jules and James were already there waiting in line. Carly reflexively tried to smooth her hair down and look a little less beach-disheveled. Darcy elbowed her in her side and wiggled her eyebrows at her while making a face.

Carly gave her a wide-eyed face that said *"Seriously stop it!"* before either Jules or James noticed that they had arrived. After they ordered their food and found a table that could seat all five of them, Carly found herself sitting across from James with Darcy sitting directly next to him. Throughout the meal, they all chatted about their beach day plans, the weather, their mutual friends, and other light topics, but James rarely laid eyes on Carly despite her frequently looking at him while he was speaking.

Each time she made eye contact with Darcy, Darcy would give her a mischievous smile or make a funny face, and in all her nervous jitters, Carly found herself laughing more than usual.

When lunch was over, Jules and James got into his car to drive to the beach parking lot. James' car had been loaded down with firewood so the girls still had to walk back to the beach.

On the walk back to their beach spot, Jill and Darcy had whispered a few things to each other before looking at Carly as if to say "Well, didn't we tell you?"

"He didn't even look at me, and honestly, I think your suspicions are way off. He probably just wanted a reason to get out of going snowboarding with the other crazy guys who are adrenaline junkies." Carly said and she honestly believed it herself, which made her a little sad.

Carly had seen when a guy was into her enough times to know. It was always so obvious. She knew guys thought she was hot, and she could usually sense their admiration pretty quickly. They would look at her in a certain way, try to get and keep her attention, and in general, were flattering and constantly trying to touch her. James was none of these, and it was a little depressing to think that her stomach had been fluttering about the thought of him all day when he was this coolly composed around her. She thought after their conversation a few days ago that maybe they would become better friends. He seemed to be letting her into his world, but today made it clear in her mind that she was just seen as his sister's friend, nothing more.

When they all met back up at the beach, Carly noticed for the first time that Jill and Darcy were wearing pretty modest tankinis while she was wearing her latest bikini purchase. She had never been ashamed of her body or felt the need to wear a modest swimsuit, but when Jules took off her swim cover and was also wearing a modest tankini, she suddenly felt out of place. Carly made up her mind to keep her tank top on for the rest of the day. It was probably silly of her, but she felt like she blended in with the other girls better that way, and she desperately wanted to fit in.

James had just come walking up carrying a tarp tied up like a sack full of wood. He plopped the heavy load down by the firepit which already had two boxes of wood sitting next to it.

"I think this will be enough firewood for the night, but my dad insisted they bring more when they come later this evening," he said pointing to the large pile of firewood.

"We were planning on getting some more boogie boarding in. You guys ready to go swimming yet?" Darcy said cheerfully.

"Yes! Just let me set up my towel area and put some more sunscreen on my shoulders. I did it before we left, but I usually burn easily. Carly, can you help me?" Jules said.

Carly had been standing right beside Jules and was able to quickly grab the can of sprayable sunscreen and give her shoulders a spritz.

Jules turned around and said "Thanks. Do you need to reapply anywhere?"

Carly laughed, "Actually, I don't think I applied sunscreen at all today." She confessed as she took the proffered can and began spraying herself all over.

"What!? Jules said in astonishment. "How have you not burned already?"

Darcy laughed, "You forget gringa, Carly is half Mexican, she doesn't burn as easily as you do."

Carly just laughed at Darcy. "We were only here for less than two hours and we were in the water for a lot of it. I definitely need sunscreen in general, I just forgot today. I guess my mind has been on other things." Carly hoped they would all assume she meant her dad, and not James who was currently shirtless and reorganizing the wood pile so it was neat and tidy.

Jill looked at Carly and then back at James. It seemed to go unnoticed by Jules however, who took the opportunity to ask Carly how her dad was doing.

"He's a bit better. His lungs still need to recover and his broken bones will take time, but he is stable and out of the coma. All in all, the doctors seem really optimistic and think he will make a full recovery in no time," Carly said with hope.

James clapping and brushing his hand off, walked over to the girls and said "I'm glad he's doing better and is out of the coma. That must be a big relief to your family." As he spoke Carly noticed that he didn't look at her. Like he was too scared to make eye contact or something.

"Well, I think the sunscreen has probably dried by now, let's go boogie boarding for a while," Carly said. She felt as though the awkward silence after James spoke would ruin a perfectly wonderful day.

The five of them boogie-boarded for hours, only stopping every now and then to reapply sunscreen at Jules' directions and allow it to dry. They also snacked on chips and soda while they took their fifteen-minute breaks from the water as Jill had informed them the sunscreen needed that long to "fully dry."

Finally, James noticed that there were others at their bonfire pit and motioned for all the girls to come take a look.

"It's not my parents, and I don't think it's any of yours. Who is that?" he asked, squinting up at the beach.

"Only one way to find out," said Darcy as she put her board over her head and started to walk up to the bonfire pit. The others followed and soon learned that it was Eric and a couple of guys from the church snowboarding trip.

"Hey, we came early and thought it would be fun to get some surfing in before the party tonight," Eric said enthusiastically. Carly noticed that all of the guys were holding cans of energy drinks. Clearly, the adrenaline from rushing down a mountainside at top speed on a tiny snowboard, wasn't enough to make up for the utter lack of sleep they had probably gotten last night.

Jill ran up and gave Eric a big hug. "I thought you guys would be late for dinner! How did you make it back so fast?" she said, grinning up at him.

"Well, to be honest. There wasn't a lot of snow and we ran out of mountain pretty fast. I guess in the summertime they only pump the two main slopes with man-made snow. All the good slopes though were hiking trails at this point. We got bored after about two hours."

"Bummer! I'm sorry it wasn't as fun as you hoped, but I'm glad you guys came early. Do you need to put on sunscreen or do you want to go get in the water?" Jill asked, still standing very close to Eric.

Eric took a swig of his energy drink. "I think we just need to chug these and then we are ready. Right guys?" he said taking yet another large gulp before belching.

They guys chuckled. A short, stalky teenager Carly hadn't met yet spoke up, "Any of you guys play volleyball?"

There was a cheer from the group, it turned out most of them loved the idea of a round of beach volleyball.

As they made their way down to the water's edge, Carly noticed that James was standing next to her and had been staring at her.

"Everything OK?" she asked him.

James looked into her eyes for the first time that day. "Yeah, why?"

"Well, I know I haven't known you for very long and I definitely don't have you figured out, but you just seemed quieter than I thought you would be," Carly said with a shrug.

It was easy to talk without the others noticing since they were all busily talking about the guys' trip to the mountains and the sounds of crashing waves made it hard to hear anything that wasn't being yelled.

James stopped walking for a moment and just kicked his foot through the sand. "I haven't told anyone what I told you at church on Wednesday," he said with a worried expression.

Carly felt stunned that this guy she barely knew would tell her he felt like a murderer when he never confessed that to anyone else. Her eyes went wide in surprise.

"Everyone knows I was driving the car and that we were both in it when my brother died, they just don't know the full story. That I was angry, and that I ran the red light, and that it was all my fault." He looked down again as if trying to regain composure.

Carly put her hand on James' arm, "I wouldn't have told anyone about it," she said gently. "I know what it's like to have parts of your life you would rather never let anyone know about."

James looked intently into her eyes and seemed on the verge of saying something when Jill called out, "You two gonna play or what?!"

The moment was over. Carly instantly dropped her hand off James' arm and ran towards the others to join the circle. James was right behind her.

The rest of the beach day was a blast, even though Carly was disappointed that Darcy had been wrong about James' motives for wanting to see her. Carly did her best to enjoy the day she had been given and get to know the guys her best friends were dating. By the time the sun was going down, there was an abundance of hotdogs, smores, singing, and laughter. Carly felt as though she had never experienced true joy in her life until that day. It was as if God was telling her that life in his kingdom meant moments of pure bliss with others who were also in the kingdom. She felt for the first time that she belonged, that she wasn't pretending to be happy just to fit in or not ruin the mood for her best friends. She was actually happy, and she knew this moment would be permanently etched into her memory.

Chapter 18: Born Again

After a week, Carly's dad was released from the hospital. His lungs, bruises, cuts, and broken bones were healing at record speed. His doctor had even mentioned that it was a miracle his injuries were as minor as they were and that more of his organs weren't damaged from the accident. Carly knew in her heart that Jesus had protected her dad, and had in fact used what looked like a terrible situation to bring them all closer together. She could see that the accident had actually helped her see her need to surrender the misery of her heart over to Jesus and take up his light-hearted gift of salvation.

The night that her dad was released from the hospital was a Wednesday, and so Carly had been allowed to skip work that night as well. She rejoiced that Shellie and Nick said she could take Joey to church while they got Nick settled back home and rested.

The following week, Carly moved back home with her mom. Heidi had been more irritable and biting lately, and Carly had the suspicion that it was because she had been so happy living with her dad's family. When Carly had plopped her bags down on her bed and sat in their small living room with her, Heidi said irritably "I thought you would just come back for your stuff. It seemed like you were planning on living with your dad forever."

"I had thought about it," Carly confessed. "But they don't have any room for me and honestly, I was worried you would be too lonely without me." She gave her mother a winsome smile.

Heidi seemed stunned by Carly's honest and straightforward response. They usually used sarcasm and verbal grenades to talk about important things, and Carly knew her response was just one result of her feeling washed clean by Jesus.

After a pause, Heidi whispered, "I was lonely while you were gone. I missed you so much." She wiped a tear away from her face abruptly.

Carly went over to the armchair her mother sat in and wrapped her arms around her. "I missed you too Mom."

After hugging her mother for a minute, Heidi's arms finally wrapped around Carly in return. Carly smiled. It had been so long since she and her mother had hugged just for the sake of hugging. She kissed her mother's wet cheek and said, "I love you Mom" before letting go.

As she sat back down on the couch, Heidi looked at her with wide eyes. "Something is very different about you. What happened while you were at your dad's?"

Carly told her mom the story of how she had come to know Jesus and given her life to him. She told her about how Jesus had rescued her from her misery, and had replaced her bitterness with peace. After talking late into the night, Carly told her mom that she would no longer be able to work on Wednesday nights because she needed to prioritize her relationship with Jesus. She understood if that meant she needed to step down altogether as a supervisor and was willing to either take a pay cut to be just a crew member or to quit entirely, whichever her mother thought would be best.

Carly had thought her mother would yell and scream at her as she had done in the past. She was preparing herself to be called "ungrateful" and "irresponsible," but those words never came.

"I think we can work something out. Irma from one of the other teams was telling me that she needs to work part-time because her kids have sports on Tuesdays and Thursdays that she has to be able to pick them up from. I think I can get her to cover your Wednesday shifts as a supervisor. In fact, I might even try to go to this church with you... if you go on Sundays. I want to see the place that has you feeling so much peace."

Carly looked at her mother's face to try and detect any irony or hidden meaning, but she seemed genuine. So Carly said, "It's not really the place I want to introduce you to Mom; it's Jesus who gives me peace, and I can't wait to take you to church to learn more about him."

The next Wednesday, Carly drove to her dad's house to pick up Joey and take him to church. Her mom had attended with her the previous Sunday and had even started reading the Bible that the church had given her as part of the Welcome Bag they handed out to new attendees. Carly marveled at how just a few months ago she had felt alone and unloved, and now she was realizing that she wasn't as isolated as she had believed. She praised Jesus for the depth of the relationships she was able to have with her parents and brother because he had set her free from the chains of shame, condemnation, bitterness, and resentment. She still fought with her mom on occasion, but Carly was learning to be gentler and more compassionate, and the impact that was having on her mom was profound.

Several weeks had passed since the Senior Skip Day beach trip, and Carly and her best friends had all graduated high school. They had been attending church together on Sunday mornings as well as

Wednesday nights for the past seven weeks. On this Sunday, Carly was facing the congregation of her church. Nick, Shellie, Joey, and her mom, Heidi, were all dressed in their Sunday best, sitting together in the front row as Carly nervously shared her testimony from the stage.

With a shaking voice, Carly read the testimony she had typed out.

"I used to think that because of my sins and the trauma that had been done to me, I would never experience joy or happiness ever again. I used to try and pretend to laugh or enjoy the moment so that I could fit in with my friends, but I never really experienced happiness. Before I gave my life to Christ, I was too miserable to find joy in anything. I saw myself as powerless, and a victim to my circumstances. I had no hope that things would ever change for me, or that I could ever be anything different. I wanted my life to be different. I wanted to be happy, but I was trapped by my own bitterness, anger, and resentment. When I first came to this church, Mrs. Carlile gave me my first Bible and told me that Jesus had told her to do it. I thought she had made a mistake or was possibly senile and crazy."

Several church members chuckled at Carly's admission including Mrs. Carlile, who was beaming up at her.

"But now I see that God was working through her to offer me the gift of salvation from my miserable way of living, and because of her faithful act of obedience and that of my best friends, I am standing here today a changed person. Jesus showed me that I was not powerless and that I have the power to choose to be a victim or a victor. I have the power to offer forgiveness to the people Satan used to try and destroy my life because I deserved to be set free from the harm they committed in my past. I have the power to choose to walk in the abundant life Jesus died to offer me. I have the power to choose joy today, even when my past is filled with tears and trials. Because of Jesus, I am happy for the first time in my life that I can remember. I know that he loves me and is working all things out for my good, and my relationships with my friends and family have never been better. Giving my heart to Jesus was the best thing that ever happened to me, and I'm so thankful that I get to spend eternity with my Lord and Savior."

Carly set down her printed testimony and stepped into the large inflatable pool the church put on stage once a month for the purpose of baptisms. The youth pastor, Dillan, was standing in the pool ready to help her in and baptize her.

Dillan said, "Carly we are so proud of your commitment to the Lord, and in front of all these witnesses I ask you to confirm the faith you have. Do you confess before all these witnesses that you have accepted Jesus as your personal Lord and Savior?"

"I do."

"Do you trust in Jesus and him alone for your salvation?"

"I do."

"Carly, I have the great pleasure to baptize you in the name of the Father, Son, and Holy Spirit."

Pastor Dillan handed his mic to an assistant before he plunged Carly into the tepid waters signifying that she was burying her old dead life, and bringing her up out of the waters to signify that she had been born again as a new person.

As Carly rose out of the water, the church erupted in cheers. Joyful clapping, yelps, and whistles went up and she got to see her dad wipe a tear from his eye with his good arm. Her mom looked like she was trying not to cry and Shellie was beaming while Joey clapped and jumped up and down. Carly looked next to them to see Jill and Darcy also clapping and jumping up and down and she had to laugh as she threw her hands up in the air in jubilant victory.

Carly was handed a towel and she exited the stage to go to the dressing room where she could change out of her wet baptism clothes

Epilogue

Carly had been going to Grace Covenant Church every week for the past seven months. Her yellow Bible was now full of highlights, underlined verses, and cramped handwritten notes in the margins. Her yellow journal that Mrs. Carlile had given her was stowed in a drawer in her desk, and she had a new journal that was almost halfway filled. Carly had just finished writing a paper for her English class in the library when she began to pack up her laptop and backpack to head back to the dorms. As she looked up, she saw James sitting at a table just ten feet away from her.

When she walked closer to his table, James looked up and Carly smiled brightly. "How is it that I had no clue you went here?" she asked him in a loud whisper.

She felt her stomach flutter a little as it always did when she saw James at church or a social gathering for the college kids. He had been keeping his distance from her for a while though and was good at making it feel impossible for her to get to know him any better. Eventually, she had just stopped trying to be his friend and accepted that they would be acquaintances only.

James smiled up at her in surprise. "I don't know. I guess it just never came up," he said in his own audible whisper.

"Well, it's nice to see a friendly face," Carly said as she adjusted her heavy bag on her shoulder. Carly was just about to walk away when James stood up and caught hold of her hand.

"Hey wait!" he said, forgetting to whisper.

Carly looked around as several annoyed heads popped up from laptops and books.

"I was just finishing up in a minute, what are you up to right now?" James asked in a whisper while letting go of Carly's wrist.

"I'm done for the day. I was going to drop my bag off in my dorm and head to the dining hall for dinner," Carly responded.

"How 'bout you wait while I pack up my bag, and I take you to this amazing pizza place that isn't too far from here so we can catch up?" James said as he quickly began shoving things into his backpack.

Carly could barely believe what she was hearing. For months this guy had avoided her and seemed to actually be trying to get away from her. Now he had grabbed her wrist, and was asking her to eat dinner with him, alone! Her heart was pounding, but she told herself to play it cool. *This might mean nothing to him.*

"James, I literally see you every Sunday," Carly said with a grin.

James was hastily packing up his stuff. "Yes, but we never seem to make it past the 'Hey, good morning, how are you? I'm fine,'" he said mockingly.

Carly covered her mouth to try and stifle a laugh. "You're right. Pizza does sound good, and to be honest, the dining hall food isn't all that great. It reminds me of cafeteria lunches from high school."

"Perfect. I'm ready," James said as he grabbed Carly's hand and the two walked out holding hands.

Carly looked down in amazement that James, the guy she had had a crush on for most of the year, was now talking to her and holding her hand.

James looked down at their clasped hands. "Sorry, is this OK? I guess I got a little carried away."

Carly's mouth had gone dry, so she just nodded.

"I have been wanting to do this for so long, it just never seemed like the right time," James admitted.

Carly stopped in her tracks and gaped at him. "You have been avoiding talking to me for at least seven months!" she blurted.

James blushed and looked down sheepishly. "I know. But let me take you out for pizza and I'll explain everything. I promise."

Carly gazed into his deep blue eyes. They were so earnest and soulful. How could she resist his invitation? "I do want to hear what you have to say."

She slipped her hand back into his as they walked to his car.

Carly's stomach was alight with flutters, and she knew that she wanted to spend the rest of her life holding his hand.

About the author

Annie Hutchison battled with mental illness for over 20 years before she was miraculously healed from a disorder with no known cure. In 2022, Annie published her first book, a fusion of memoir and self-help titled, Through Dark Places: The Life Lessons and Spiritual Disciplines that Enable Miraculous Healing. Annie is passionate about writing content that inspires others to seek Jesus so that they too can find the only true source of healing. When Annie isn't busy writing, she enjoys reading, playing games with her family, gardening, baking, and taking care of her chickens.

To read more by Annie, please visit www.anniehutchison.com